REASON TO KILL

"I think Big Jim and Little Jim were behind it," Wild said.

"Yeah," Ness said. "The two Jims. And I'd bet a year's pay that Harry Gibson, their out-of-work, one-man goon squad, is wielding that tommy gun for 'em."

Wild lit up another Lucky. "What will you do?"

"All I can do is put them in jail," Ness said, digging his hands into his topcoat pockets. "Or hope they resist arrest when I come to pick them up."

"So you have a reason to kill them?"

Ness smiled faintly. "I already have a reason," he said. "It's an excuse I'm looking for."

*Further Eliot Ness Titles by Max Allan Collins
from Severn House*

THE DARK CITY
BULLET PROOF

BULLET PROOF

An Eliot Ness Novel

by

Max Allan Collins

This title first published in Great Britain 2005 by
SEVERN HOUSE PUBLISHERS LTD of
9–15 High Street, Sutton, Surrey SM1 1DF.
This first hardcover edition published in the USA 2006 by
SEVERN HOUSE PUBLISHERS INC of
595 Madison Avenue, New York, N.Y. 10022.

British Library Cataloguing in Publication Data

Collins, Max Allan
    The dark city. - (An Eliot Ness mystery)
    1.   Ness, Eliot - Fiction
    2.   Organized crime - Ohio - Cleveland - Fiction
    3.   Government investigators - Fiction
    4.   Cleveland (Ohio) - History - Fiction
    5.   Suspense fiction
    I.   Title
    813.5'4 [F]

    ISBN 0-7278-6298-7

Printed and bound in Great Britain by
MPG Books Ltd., Bodmin, Cornwall.

*This novel is dedicated to the memory of
my friend and Dick Tracy collaborator
John Locher
1961–1986*

ONE

July 27–September 13, 1937

1

Eliot Ness stepped out on the balcony of his office and surveyed the angry mob below, facing what was any public official's worst nightmare with an expression as placid as a priest's.

Despite the sweltering late afternoon, they swarmed the City Hall sidewalk, perhaps fifteen hundred men and women, strikers from the steel mills, many with their wives in tow, children too, jammed together tighter than their anger. A banner said: THE POLICE CAN'T BREAK THIS STRIKE! Another said: BRING ON YOUR MILITIA! Someone spotted Ness, out on his perch, and a wave of outrage rolled across an already turbulent sea of humanity.

Ness nodded at them and smiled faintly, waving, popelike, as if the booing had been cheers, then ducked back inside. His smile disappeared; the sound of displeasure behind him—muffled now as he shut the balcony doors—did not.

Cleveland's Director of Public Safety was, at thirty-four, the youngest such officer in any major city in the United States. But right now he felt anything but young. He moved to one of the conference tables that took up most of the floor space of his ample office, a masculine room of dark wood and pebbled glass, where three men stood, their eyes on him like magnets on metal. He sat on the edge of the table, his casual posture at odds with his crisply tailored, double-breasted brown suit with its green-and-yellow striped knit tie and flourish of a tan silk breast-pocket handkerchief. His boyish face seemed devoid of

3

any thought or emotion, save for an inch-long crease between his dark eyebrows.

Earlier today more than one thousand steel strikers, blocking entrances to Republic Steel's Corrigan-McKinney plant in the industrial Flats, had done battle with one hundred reserves from the Cleveland police department. Bricks had flown, billy clubs flailed.

Ness brushed a comma of dark hair off his forehead and said, "I'd like a complete status report."

The three men pulled their eyes off Ness and bounced worried glances off each other.

One of the men was Chief of Police George Matowitz, a heavy-set six-footer in his mid-fifties with a wide, florid face, tiny blue eyes darting behind wire-frame glasses; the chief's uniform was, as usual, freshly pressed, his silver badge gleaming on his broad chest.

"How can you send my boys out there without guns?" Matowitz said, more confused than angry. "I've got two men in the hospital."

"How many strikers are in the hospital?"

"Six," Matowitz said, shrugging.

Until Ness came along a year and a half ago and began shaking up the police department, weeding out the rotten apples, raising the qualifications for cops, ending the patronage system, Matowitz had been riding his desk, waiting for retirement. Not a corrupt cop, in fact known for his doggedness and bravery in his younger days as a detective, Matowitz had for years been content to look the other way while high-ranking officers made themselves rich and the department a joke.

But ever since Ness rattled his cage, Chief Matowitz had been taking a more active role; if less than a go-getter, he had been more than cooperative.

He reminded Ness of that fact: "I've backed you all the way, Mr. Ness. Through hell and high water . . . your policies aren't exactly prized by every cop on the department, you know."

"They're not alone," Ness said, nodding toward the murmur of disapproval beyond the balcony doors. Smiling faintly again, he added, "I guess the honeymoon is over."

"Hell," Robert Chamberlin said wryly, thumbs looped in his vest pockets, "I'm beginning to question the marriage."

A lanky but broad-shouldered man in his late thirties, Chamberlin was the safety director's executive assistant, a lawyer handpicked by Ness to handle both administrative and investigative duties. His oblong, sharp-featured face was dominated by a shovel jaw and a tiny black mustache, and his dark hair was slicked back on a high forehead.

"The objective of this job," Ness told his assistant gently, "isn't winning popularity contests."

"Isn't it, Eliot?" Chamberlin asked, not so gently. "I'd say your popularity in this city has a great bearing on what you can get away with."

The other two men said nothing; Chamberlin was, after all, the only one of them who was comfortable calling the safety director by his first name.

"Go on," Ness said.

"You've got a good reputation in this town. People know you aren't afraid to throw crooked cops in jail, or to buck the local politicos. You kick doors down and collar bad guys; you—"

"Make your point, Bob."

"The point is, nobody's dead yet. Look at what's happening in strikes in other cities right now. I think you can keep the violence here down to a minimum, but you need to get into the game personally."

"Go out there to Corrigan-McKinney myself, you mean."

"Exactly."

"Then you approve of my directive."

"Limiting our boys to nightsticks and tear gas? No guns? You're damned right I approve."

Matowitz was shaking his head like a bear ducking bees. "No, no, no," he said. "You have to take a *stand*. You got to side with our boys."

"And which side are our boys on, Chief?"

"Well . . . we got to back Republic Steel, Mr. Ness."

"Not the strikers? Aren't they citizens?"

"Well, of course they are. But they're citizens break-ing the law!"

"Albert," Ness said, turning to the third man, "did you look into that union-hall incident?"

"Yes, I did," Albert Curry said. "And it's vandalism, all right."

Curry, a pale, cherubic man in his late twenties, was a detective assigned to the safety director's office. He repre-sented, to Ness, the sort of young, honest, well-trained, idealistic officer that Cleveland, and every big city, needed, if police departments were to be dragged screaming and kicking into the twentieth century.

"Then the steel workers' headquarters really was turned upside down, as their people say?"

"Oh yes," Curry said. "Broken windows, smashed dishes, overturned tables, cracked chairs, shattered lamps—"

"And they didn't do it themselves, obviously."

"No. They say it was 'hired gangsters and company police.'"

"If that's true," Ness said, gazing significantly at Matowitz, "then Republic's breaking the law, too."

"I don't know the facts," Matowitz said, reddening, "but I can understand a company hiring on a little outside help for security reasons."

"Security is one thing," Ness said. "Goons are another."

"If you're intending to take the side of the strikers—"

"I intend to take the side of the city," Ness said. He checked his watch. "If you'll excuse me, gentlemen, I have a meeting with the mayor."

Curry and Chamberlin nodded and took seats at one of the conference tables; but Matowitz trailed along after Ness, saying, "It's going to be very dangerous, when night falls. You have to let me arm my boys."

"No," Ness said. Their footsteps echoed off the mar-ble floor of the open hallway beyond the railing of which rose the City Hall atrium. Standing at attention, just outside the mayor's office, were eight uniformed, armed police officers. Ness glanced at Matowitz, looking for an explanation.

"I've appointed these men the Mayor's Guard. In a situation this dangerous, I thought it wise to—"

"They're not needed, Chief." Ness turned to the cops and said, "Go downstairs. You can keep an eye on the entrances, if you like, but don't go out on the street. You'd just incite a riot."

"What in hell do you call what's going on out there now?" Matowitz said huffily, gesturing toward the outside.

"I call it a peaceful assemblage, but we could turn it into a riot if we wanted to. Do you want to, Chief?"

"Well... of course not."

Ness put his hand on Matowitz's shoulder. "I know it's hard to have your own in the hospital. But don't forget: that's largely what those people out there are upset about, themselves."

Matowitz sighed and stayed out in the hall, going to the railing to watch his Mayor's Guard disperse below, while Ness moved through the outer office, getting a nod from the mayor's male secretary to go on in.

Harold Burton was an unpretentious sort of man to be working out of an office called, aptly, the Tapestry Room. Five huge tapestries depicting the Indian days of the Western Reserve draped the finely detailed, oak-paneled walls; the ceiling was high and ornately-sculptured plaster; a massive wood-and-stone fireplace provided a mantel for a multitude of framed family photos. Burton was, after all, a homey sort, devoted to his wife and children, a man who looked more like a farmer than a big-city mayor.

A powerfully built, wedge-shaped man of fifty years and medium height, Burton's broad brow and regular features were made memorable only by dark-circled eyes; he looked almost haunted today, and, typically, borderline disheveled: his brown suit rumpled, his dark tie food-stained.

He stood behind his desk, gesturing for his safety director to sit in one of four chairs opposite him; then the mayor sat as well, saying, "We're going to be joined in about five minutes by representatives of the Steel Workers Organizing Committee. Any objection?"

"None," Ness said. He sat slightly slumped in the chair, legs crossed, ankle on knee.

"You've held the violence to a minimum thus far," said Burton, "and you're to be commended. But I'm afraid if we can't get these fellas to listen to reason, we're in for some bloodshed."

"There doesn't have to be."

"There already has been. Eight people in the hospital."

"And they may have company, before the day's out. But there's not going to be any shooting."

Burton nodded slowly. "No guns. You think your people can control the situation that way?"

"Yes."

"I know someone who disagrees."

"And who would that be?"

"Girdler."

Ness laughed mirthlessly. "Republic's chairman. When did Mr. Girdler make this observation?"

"Not five minutes ago." Burton gestured to one of several phones on his desk. "He didn't come calling, he *called* . . . he declined to go wading through the thousand or two folks expressing their discontent out on our sidewalk."

"What was Girdler's complaint, exactly?"

"That we're too soft. That you are too soft."

"Oh really. Excuse me if I bust out crying."

Burton grinned as he withdrew a big black Havana from a plain wooden box on his desk; he lit up the cigar, puffing, enjoying it like a hungry man would a banquet, and said, "He thinks it's insane for your men to go into battle unarmed."

"Maybe I don't particularly crave a battle."

His grin settling into a vaguely sarcastic smile, Burton gestured with his cigar and said, "He wants to bring in the National Guard. He's been talking to Governor Davey."

"Really. I would think that would be your prerogative."

"I would think the same."

"And are you?"

"Going to call in the militia? No. Not as long as things stay under control."

Ness straightened in the chair. "There are people on both sides who would like to see this escalate into a war, you know."

The intercom on Burton's desk buzzed, and his secretary informed him of the arrival of the SWOC representatives.

"Send them in," Burton said, reluctantly putting out his cigar.

Three men entered. One of them, a stocky, world-weary man of perhaps forty, wore a suit and tie; the other two wore work shirts and slacks, one of them lean, hawk-faced, dark, the other burly, square-headed, fair. The latter two, the working men, glanced dourly about the high-ceilinged, ostentatious chamber as if wondering whether to feel intimidation or mistrust. All three planted themselves just behind the chairs opposite Burton's desk, putting a wall between them and Burton and Ness, who stood to greet them.

"I'm George Owens," the stocky man said, gesturing to a hand-painted tie with a sunset on it. His voice was rough and so were his features, gray eyes squinting skeptically out of pouches of flesh. "I'm from the national office of the SWOC. John L. Lewis himself sent me in to advise and counsel these men."

Republic Steel would characterize Owens as an "outside agitator," Ness knew; and perhaps he was.

Burton said, "Pleased to meet you, Mr. Owens," and extended his hand.

Owens swallowed carefully, like the food-taster for an unpopular king, then stepped forward, past the barricade of the chairs, and shook Burton's hand.

"This is Eliot Ness," Burton said, "the Director of Public Safety."

"Mr. Owens," Ness said, and nodded, and offered his hand.

Owens shook it, firmly, looking at Ness with open suspicion. The hand was rough from manual labor, Ness noted; this meant Owens was not an attorney, which was a relief.

"These gentlemen represent the local strike committee," Owens said. "Alex Ballin and Harold Selby."

The two men stepped around the chairs, awkwardly, to shake hands with Ness and Burton, and then Burton asked them to sit down. Ballin, the hawk-faced one, seemed ill at ease and said little, though he was obviously bubbling with anger. Selby was less stoic, but just as angry.

"We want to know," Owens said, "whether your administration is on the side of Republic Steel, or intends to be fair to its citizens who are trying to protect their rights to their jobs."

"The latter, of course," Burton said.

Owens paid no attention to that, pressing on. "We demand an immediate investigation of Republic Steel for importing strike breakers. We demand that the police department shut down Corrigan-McKinney because Republic Steel has violated the law."

"No," Burton said flatly. "I have no right to do that."

Selby, sitting forward, biting off words, said, "Republic is importing scabs from Pennsylvania, Canada, and God-knows-where. Is that fair?"

"Certainly not," Burton said. "But I'm powerless to prevent that. Personally, I think the work should go to Clevelanders . . . but I doubt you feel much brotherly love toward our local 'scabs,' either."

Selby was almost shouting now. "Your cops destroyed our picket tent this morning, smashed a radio—"

Burton held two fingers in the air and said, "I have two police officers in the hospital." Then he raised three fingers on either hand. "You have six strikers similarly indisposed. What do you propose we do to keep the casualties at this level?"

"*You* attacked *us!*" Selby said.

Owens patted the air hard, a gesture at once calming and impatient, and Selby's lips tightened into a line; then Owens looked sharply at Burton and said, "Your cops waded into our pickets with billy clubs. Pushed our people off the picket line, forced them down Broadway, way the hell away from the plant entrances."

Ness said, "Strikers were hurling bricks at trucks and cars taking nonstrikers into the plant. My understanding is that a mounted police officer rode into the crowd, going after a picket brandishing a brick, and was knocked off his horse. *That's* when the other officers 'waded' in."

Hawk-faced Ballin spoke up: "Those bricks were thrown by men planted among us by the company."

Ness raised an eyebrow. "My assistant, Robert Chamberlin, was down there this morning. He was threatened by strikers with bricks; and they were local people. This violence cuts both ways, gentlemen."

"What do you propose to do about it?" Owens said coldly.

"Anyone throwing bricks at cars will be arrested," Ness said, shrugging. "If it's somebody the company planted, then I guess we'll find out."

"What about the trashing of our union hall?" Selby demanded. "That was company thugs who did that!"

"I'm investigating that. If Republic hired that done, we'll prosecute."

"Why should we trust you?" Selby asked.

"Because my men haven't shot anybody," Ness said. "And they are not going to. Or would you prefer I provide you with a few martyrs, Mr. Owens? I know Republic Steel would appreciate it if I would throw some lead around, and scare your people back to work."

Burton winced at that, but said, "We are not here to take sides, gentlemen."

"We're here to keep the peace," Ness added quickly. "Now what do *you* propose to do toward that end?"

Owens shook his head side to side. "We're on strike. We don't expect it to be easy."

"Then why are you wasting our time?" Ness snapped. "If you want a bloodbath, don't expect me to aid and abet you, and then take the rap for you, too. I won't play savior for you, and I won't play villain, either. If you want to avoid more violence, then limit the number of your pickets and don't physically try to stop nonstrikers from entering the plant."

"Scabs," Ballin said bitterly.

"Not necessarily," Burton said, gesturing with an open hand. "This morning I had a call from Walter L. Wonder, who is chairman of the Republic Employee's Association . . ."

"Company union," Selby snorted.

". . . and he claims twenty-two hundred of the thirty-eight hundred employed at Corrigan-McKinney are not on strike."

Owens laughed at that. "That's utterly fantastic. We have better than fifty percent of Corrigan-McKinney, and more joining us daily."

"Then strike peacefully," Ness said, "and wait for the company to come around."

"You want us to limit our pickets," Selby said, eyes burning. "Well, why don't you reduce your damn cops at the mill?"

"The number of officers on duty," Ness said, "will reflect the need, as the emergency requires."

"Why don't you present your grievances to the police," Burton suggested, gesturing gently, "instead of bucking them?"

Owens rolled his eyes, stood; he sighed theatrically. Made a show of looking about the Tapestry Room, from ornate ceiling to plushly carpeted floor. Then he smiled a smile that had nothing to do with happiness and said, "We're not getting anywhere. It's clear where you stand. But I would think that even from this ivory tower you could get a view of what's going on down in the real world—on your City Hall sidewalk, for instance." He nodded to the other two men, said, "Boys," and together they stalked out, Owens in the lead.

Burton and Ness sat in silence. The mayor sighed heavily, lit another Havana and said, "What about tonight?"

Ness looked at his watch. "When the eleven P.M. shift goes on, that's when all hell will break loose."

"What do you propose we do about it?"

"I don't know what you're going to do about it," Ness said, rising, "but I'm going to be there to catch it."

And he left the mayor there to ponder that, while he went to his office to get Albert Curry, Bob Chamberlin, and a gun.

2

Detective Albert Curry, behind the wheel of the black Ford sedan with the special EN-1 license plate, didn't know what to make of the situation. Or, to be more exact, he didn't know what to make of the way his chief was behaving in this situation.

Curry had great admiration for Ness, who had in little more than a year made enormous strides toward cleaning up Cleveland's almost impossibly corrupt police department. Not to mention the safety director's record prior to coming to Cleveland, a record in law enforcement second to few in the nation, second to none when you considered his age.

A prohibition agent in Chicago, assigned to the Justice Department and later Treasury, Ness and his small, hand-picked squad—known in the press as the "untouchables," due to their resistance to bribes, threats, and politics—had been instrumental in strangling the Chicago mob financially. Raiding breweries, confiscating beer trucks, seizing records, Ness and his crew earned much of the credit for sending crime kingpin Al Capone on his long ride up the river. This was followed by Ness's war against moonshiners in the mountains (and mobsters in the cities) of Kentucky, Tennessee, and Ohio, which proved similarly successful and publicity-making, landing Ness the choice but precarious job of Cleveland's safety director.

Beyond this, Curry knew, Ness was at the forefront of modern thinking in police science and criminology, having trained at the University of Chicago under August Vollmer. With half a dozen successful crooked-cop prosecutions behind him, Ness was effecting his plan to update the force, switching over from foot patrol to patrol cars, reorganizing the traffic bureau, instituting a juvenile delinquency unit and much else.

But what impressed Curry most about Ness was not his forward thinking or administrative skills, but the tendency of the youthful safety director to get out from behind his desk and direct investigations personally. Curry was well aware that a certain amount of Ness's detective work and "derring-do" reflected the mayor's need for the former T-man to create favorable publicity—which was why the badly factionalized city council had managed to get behind this administration, where Ness's police and fire departments were concerned.

Curry knew, too, that Ness got restless when tied down to his office, that he thrived on being out in the field. It was said that Eliot Ness took no greater pleasure out of life than when he was kicking down a door and conducting a raid.

So it was no surprise to Curry to find himself driving Ness to the front lines of the volatile Republic Steel strike. What surprised Curry was seeing his chief strap on a shoulder-holstered revolver, back at Ness's City Hall office.

Despite the somewhat deserved reputation Ness had for embracing danger, Curry knew that Ness rarely ever carried a gun. "They won't be so quick to shoot at you," he had explained, "if they know you can't shoot back." And resorting to the use of a gun to resolve a situation meant failure to born-diplomat Ness.

Yet tonight Eliot Ness was carrying a gun *into* a situation. Odd, Curry thought; particularly considering the strict "no firearms" orders the police detail at Corrigan-McKinney was saddled with.

But Curry said nothing about it to Ness, who had his fedora in his lap and rode leaning against the window, gazing out almost dreamily at the blush of red against the sky that was the signature of the steel mills.

"On summer nights," Ness said, "we used to sit out on the porch and drink beer and watch the sky turn orange."

"Sir?"

Ness smiled gently without looking at Curry. "South Side of Chicago, where I grew up," he explained. "Roseland was my neighborhood . . . so close to the mills that if you faced east, you'd see an incredible glow on the sky . . . especially if they were opening the steel furnaces to clean out the coke."

Curry had never heard Ness talk about Chicago, not even the Capone days, let alone anything about growing up.

"Worked in the Pullman plant," he continued, "when I got out of high school. Dipping radiators. Hard work. I don't envy these men their lives."

"The question is," Bob Chamberlin said from the backseat, "do you begrudge them a pay raise?"

Ness stared out the window. Enough time had elapsed to make Curry think there would be no response to Chamberlin's question when Ness said quietly, "That's not my decision." Then a beat later: "I wish it were."

Curry understood his chief's sympathies for the strikers, if not the contradiction of the gun under Ness's arm. Curry came from a working-class neighborhood himself, on Cleveland's far east side. His father—a skilled cabinet-maker sixty years of age—had been laid off two years ago by the furniture company that employed him for twenty-eight years. Curry, and his brother John, who also had a job with the city, were covering their parents' mortgage payments; his father—a life-long Republican who'd always had a hardheaded you-get-what-you-earn/you-get-out-of-life-what-you-put-into-it philosophy—was accepting fifteen dollars a month from the county relief office.

The Depression was, to Curry, some awful, arbitrary force of nature, a disaster not unlike a tornado or flood or earthquake, leaving misery and hardship in its path. Sur-

vival had become the first order of business, finding and
keeping a job the top priority.

Curry felt lucky to have a job—he'd worked hard to
get where he was with the department, but he knew he
was mostly lucky. As a traffic cop he'd pulled several
people, including a small child, from a burning car;
Ness's predecessor in the safety director's chair had
very badly needed a "brave, honest officer" (as the
papers had embarrassingly put it) as a positive example.
So Albert Curry was promoted to detective—youngest
in the city—without having to buy his badge, a rarity at
the time.

If he questioned the wisdom of those with jobs going
out on strike, in hard times, for better pay and working
conditions, he understood their mistrust of company
owners. At General Motors in Flint, Michigan, tycoons
making half a million dollars a year had paid twenty
cents an hour to the men on the line until, last year,
sit-down strikes forced GM's surrender. With FDR back
in the White House, sympathetic to the union cause,
now was the time (some said) for the working man to
take a stand. A wave of strikes had followed GM's
capitulation, and what was happening at Corrigan-
McKinney was part of that.

Not long ago United States Steel, in order to avoid
being struck, handed its workers a ten-percent wage in-
crease, a forty-hour week, and union recognition. So-
called "Little Steel," however, the independent steel mills
of which Republic was one, wasn't about to give up so
easily.

Curry was pleased with the even-handed manner in
which his chief had responded to the strike thus far—
frustrating as it might be to the men on the line, Ness's
no-firearms decision was, in Curry's opinion, correct.

So why the gun in the shoulder holster?

His mouth dry, Curry clutched the wheel, hoping he
could do his job without compromising his sympathies for
the strikers. Sympathies he dared not express out loud . . .

Just after dark, when the crowds had abandoned the

City Hall sidewalk for home and/or the plant picket line, Curry had driven Ness over to the Central Police Station at Twenty-first and Payne, where Ness had arranged to have a newsreel sent over by the Hearst people.

Ness used a large conference room on the second floor to screen the newsreel for one hundred uniformed police, most of whom had already worked a shift today, but who at nine o'clock tonight would be replacing the detail that was working the Corrigan-McKinney gate now. Also present, at Ness's pointed request, was Chief Matowitz.

There were stirrings among the men, who were of course less than pleased by the no-firearms directive, and when Ness stood before the assemblage, he said, "I overheard a man saying that this was one hell of a time to be showing a training film. Well, gentlemen . . . this is one hell of a training film."

He nodded to Chamberlin, in back, who was manning the projector, and to Curry, who dimmed the lights, having not the slightest damn idea what this was about.

"Something happened on a field in South Chicago not long ago," Ness said quietly. "Not far from where I grew up."

And now Curry knew what Ness was up to; so did a good many of the cops in the room, but none could be prepared for the scenes that followed.

At first there was no sound other than the whirring of the sprocketed film, but then as images began to fill the screen, so did sound fill the room. It was raw footage, without any reporter doing voice-over; but no voice-over was needed.

In the midst of an open field, a parade of strikers and sympathizers—men, women, and children—encounter a wall of police; heated words are exchanged by one of the cops and the spokesman of the marchers. Suddenly the sound of gunfire rips the afternoon, and a dozen men in the front ranks of the strikers are cut down like weeds. Revolvers in hand, the police charge into the strikers; tear-gas grenades sail into the crowd, nightsticks fly.

Most of the crowd flees; a few strikers who lag behind are beaten senseless by police, sometimes two or three cops working over one striker, the manner of these public servants chillingly businesslike. A girl, not more than five feet tall, weighing perhaps one hundred pounds, is clubbed from behind by a nightstick. She staggers until thoughtful police jostle her into a paddy wagon, blood streaking her face like grotesquely smeared makeup.

For six minutes a symphony of swinging nightsticks, blasting revolvers, bleeding strikers, is played out, until, finally, the newsreel runs its course and the film flaps in the projector, like the wagging tail of a dog, anxious to please.

When the lights came up, Ness stood before them expressionless, the room bathed in silence.

"Ten strikers killed," Ness said finally. "By cops. No dead women or children, thank God, but as many people— women and children among them—as are present here were hospitalized for injuries . . . including twenty-three policemen."

No one in the room needed to be told that the newsreel's strike had occurred at a Republic Steel mill.

"And that, gentlemen," Ness said, with hard eyes and a humorless smile, "explains why you're going on duty unarmed, tonight."

A hand was raised midway back.

Ness nodded, and the cop, a young one, stood, saying, "Sir—surely you expect us to defend ourselves."

"You will have nightsticks, and some of you will have tear gas. Use these sparingly, if at all. The only weapon in your arsenal I want you to use unsparingly is good judgment."

They had filed out soberly. Matowitz waited and said something to Ness—something conciliatory, apparently, as it was followed by the two men shaking hands and exchanging warm if weary smiles.

Ness, Chamberlin, and Curry had left the police station around ten; Curry suggested to his chief that he take another car, rather than the easily recognized EN-1 sedan, but Ness said being noticed was part of the exercise.

Curry caught Broadway just south of the Central Station, trading the bustle and neon glow of the downtown for the desolate gloom of the industrial Flats, the bottomland area that was home to the twisting Cuyahoga River as well as steel mills, warehouses, and factories. For several blocks Broadway traced the edge of the bluff overlooking the Flats; then, suddenly, the street took a sharp right and dropped straight down, as if a trapdoor under the city had given way.

Soon they were driving through an ill-lit area of small factories and warehouses; and after Broadway—a well-paved, well-maintained street—bottomed out, the side street Dille, not so well-paved or maintained, cut away.

"Park along here," Ness said while they were still on Broadway, the smokestacks of the steel mill well in sight, smudging the black sky with gray smoke; a block or so down was the Dille intersection. At least several hundred strikers were gathered at the intersection, in the minimal glow of two lamp posts, blocking the way, banners and placards and flags in hand; cars were parked along Broadway, but not many. Most of these people had been brought in by truck or bus; others came on foot.

Ness, his natty brown suit looking freshly pressed despite the long day its wearer had put in, got out of the sedan and stood, keeping watch. Curry and Chamberlin got out as well; the sound of the strikers milling about was constant, like restless waves crashing up onto a beach, and screeches and crashes and metallic whines—like calls from strange birds circling that beach—drifted from the crippled but still functioning steel mill.

The mill was in a pocket of the Flats; to one side was the bluff, while on the other, the rocky, debris-strewn landscape was shared by train tracks and the winding, oily Cuyahoga and rotting, half-collapsed docks. An acrid, sooty smell mingled with the Cuyahoga's sickly bouquet. This was a clear if dark night made foggy by the mill's towering smokestacks.

Around a quarter till eleven, close to shift change, cars and several buses bearing nonstrikers began to make

their way down Broadway to the turnoff; Ness stood out in
the street a block and a half away, watching the activity, as
the rumble of strikers' discontent rose into a roar, shouts
and curses hurled like bricks at the vehicles.

But no literal bricks, Curry noted.

And the vehicles, though moving like a child through
wet sand, did make it through the clogged intersection.
The protesters made their point, but did not completely
block passage.

Relief etched a thin smile on Ness's lips; and Curry
traded Chamberlin a raised eyebrow for a shrug. Perhaps
this was as ugly as it would get tonight. Perhaps the worst
was over. Eight in the hospital was bad enough, but it was
hardly ten dead and one hundred hospitalized, the after-
math of that recent afternoon in a field in South Chicago.

Then the steam whistle blew for shift change, as loud
and piercing as Gabriel's horn, and just as unsettling, only
it wasn't heralding good news: When it let up, there was a
momentary silence followed by angry shouts, followed just
as quickly by overlapping screams of pain, of fear.

A lot of them.

Ness jumped behind the wheel of the sedan and
Chamberlin and Curry hopped in, all three men squeezing in front like Oakies in a pickup truck.

Chamberlin grinned nervously at Ness as they
approached the intersection where panic had turned the
gathered strikers into a mob, and said, "Are you still
convinced announcing ourselves with your goddamned
license plate is a swell idea?"

A brick bounced off the windshield, spiderwebbing
the glass.

"Wonder what Capone did with *his* car," Ness said
with a remote smile, the sedan crawling steadily through
the human blockade, an ever-changing array of angry faces
passing before them through the webbed glass.

"Capone?" Curry asked, surprised he could get the
word out from around the heart stuck in his throat.

"Bulletproof glass an inch thick," Ness said, hunkering

over the wheel. "Armor-plated Cadillac. Don't think the city would spring for the thirty grand, though."

The road cut sharply to the right, across the front of the looming mill, the landscape opening onto a virtual battlefield. Night near the well-lighted, smoky plant was like a murky day. At first it looked like strikers were fighting each other; cops were circulating, as best they could, attempting to break up fist fights, pulling people off of each other. The bluecoats were not, Curry was relieved to see (at least judging by what he *could* see), taking part in the melee. Bricks were flying, billy clubs slashing, fists punching, even gun butts swinging, but cops weren't doing it. Two mounted officers were so boxed in by the throng, it was all the men could do to keep their wildly neighing horses from rearing up, let alone exercise any sort of crowd control.

Shouts and screams, anger and pain, the hysterical whinnying of the horses, combined into one chaotic din. Shrill cries floated across the battlefield, bansheelike; standing up along the bluff were spectators, many of them women hugging children, the women's auxiliary of the strikers, silhouetted there, lined up along the high horizon like Indians at Little Big Horn. Only these were not warriors, waiting to swoop down, but horrified witnesses, wailing, shrieking, helpless.

Bricks and billy clubs and the heels of fists and feet smashed into the sedan as it pushed through, rocking the vehicle. Ness stopped the car, put his hand on the door latch, and Chamberlin, next to him, said, "You're not going *out* there?"

"That's why I came," he said. "Albert, you come with me, do your best to stay with me, anyway. Bob, you radio for reinforcements... and ambulances."

"Oh-kay," Chamberlin said as Ness climbed out on one running board and Curry the other.

Ness looked over the top of the car at Curry and, having to shout to be heard over the pandemonium, pointing, called, "See that sound truck?"

And above the bobbing heads of the brawlers, right

up near the front gate and the chain-link fence that was swaying as combatants fought up against it, was a green panel truck with a large sound horn atop it. Strikers often used these, Curry knew, to boom instructions out to picketers, to challenge nonstrikers and scabs as they entered a plant; but now it was strangely silent, the car swaying like the fence, getting bumped into, a buoy in a sea of fighting.

Through the jostle of panicking, angry strikers, Ness moved like a shark, Curry in his wake. Blows were swung their way, fists and billy clubs, too, but the two detectives bobbed, weaved, ducked, and when necessary deflected them with raised forearms. Curry took a billy club blow across his arm that hurt like hell, but nothing broke. Occasionally a man seemed to recognize Ness, and backed off—not afraid of him, just stunned to see him here. It took several minutes to run this gauntlet, but then they were there, up against the sound truck. Ness, his hat lost in the journey, stopped a club-wielding cop who looked confused, not knowing who—or whether—to hit.

"What the hell happened here, officer?" Ness yelled.

"When the shift changed," the cop yelled back, "guys streamed out of the plant with clubs and saps and you name it. I seen some guns, too. . . ."

Ness nodded, eyes hard, teeth clenched. He said, "Get back to it, officer. . . keep trying to break this thing up!"

The officer nodded, eyes wide with frustration and fear, and dove back into the fray.

On the driver's side of the sound truck, parked near the fence, Ness found that the vehicle was empty, either abandoned or separated from its operators. It was locked. Ness withdrew his revolver and smashed the window with the butt once, webbing it; twice, shattering it; reached in, unlocked the door, opening it. Standing on the running board, he leaned over, switched on the amplifier on the dash, turned the switch to HIGH, and pulled the hand mike on its coiled rubber cord, finding it had plenty of length.

Ness handed the mike to Curry and said, "Give this to me when I get up there."

"Up where?"

Ness didn't answer.

Curry watched, dumbfounded, as the safety director climbed atop the slightly rounded roof of the panel truck, the .38 long-barreled revolver in one hand. Once up there, he reached down to Curry and filled his other hand with the mike on the long coiled cord.

Then Eliot Ness, standing atop the sound truck, noticed by no one as yet except the tribe of women observing from the bluff, fired the revolver into the air, once. Twice. Three times. Four times.

Smoke and flame accompanied the gunfire as Ness pointed the weapon straight in the air, like another smokestack.

And everyone froze, in mid-punch, mid-billy-club swing, mid-whatever. They froze in the midst of the heat of the summer night and of battle and saw Ness standing there with his gun in his hand and an expression that would've turned Medusa to stone.

Slowly, he lowered the gun. He had their attention. He raised the microphone to his mouth, thumb clicking it on; a whine of feedback briefly cut the air. And then, as startling as the gunshots, Ness's soft voice, amplified many times, made metallic by the sound-truck system, filled the night.

"That's what you've been waiting for, isn't it?" Ness said. The soft, husky voice conveyed a world of bitterness. "Gunfire? Isn't that what you all want?"

Haunted faces stared back at him; not a word was spoken in response.

"Ten dead at the Memorial Day Massacre in Chicago. One hundred sent to the hospital. Last month, at Massillon, two strikers machine-gunned, dead where they fell."

The Massillon, Ohio, strike was yet another against Republic Steel.

"Is that what you all want?" Ness said. Voice loud and tinny. A comma of dark hair swinging across his forehead, he seemed an unmustached, benign Hitler. "To die? To bleed? For a cause? Well, not in my town you don't."

He put the gun away and he withdrew a piece of paper from his pocket. Now the crowd began to make noise, but softly, mumbling, rumbling.

"The mayor has at my request issued a proclamation, a directive," Ness said into the mike. "I'm not going to read it to you. I'm going to spare you the 'whereases' and 'therefores.' But the gist is this: starting immediately, I'm establishing a peace zone of five hundred yards around this plant. Pickets who come any closer than five hundred yards will be arrested."

A general grumbling came up.

Ness spoke over it: "Furthermore, anyone seen with any weapon—*any* weapon: brick, billy club, bat, bottle, two-by-four, rock, *any* weapon—will be arrested. This is not limited to strikers. This includes company employees. Is that understood?"

Silence blanketed the men; eyes tightened with thought; a few heads nodded yes. A few men seemed to be near smiling.

"Strikers, you need to move back at least to the intersection of Dille and Broadway."

As Ness was saying this, the sounds of sirens cut the air.

Men looked back in panic, and Ness spoke into the mike, saying, "Yes, those are reinforcements. But we also have ambulances on the way. So please step away from the injured and allow the police to handle them."

Amid grumbling, one voice stood out: "Screw the police."

"This is not South Chicago," Ness said. "This is not Massillon. My men are carrying no firearms. But you'll get your head split open, breathe tear gas, and do time in the lockup if you do not disperse, *now*."

Slowly, with much grumbling and sighing, the men began to move away from the battlefield. Cops accompanied them, including the two mounted officers, breaking it up when little scuffles and shoving matches threatened to grow into something more. Other cops bent over the injured, and there were dozens of them. Blood pooled up here and there on the gravel. Bricks, bottles, clubs, broken boards, and various makeshift weapons were strewn about.

Ambulances began pulling in, and the wounded were tended to. Four Black Marias filled with reserve cops arrived, and Ness made a human barrier of the bluecoats across the front of the plant.

Ness, Chamberlin, and Curry were standing by the sound truck when a stocky, disheveled-looking individual in a suit and tie approached. The side of his head was bloody. Curry didn't know the man, but Ness did.

"Mr. Owens," Ness said. "You obviously need some attention for that injury. Just go with the ambulance attendants, they'll—"

"I'm fine, Mr. Ness. I just want to claim my truck."

"Oh. Are you sure you're in shape to drive?"

"Yes. I've had worse than this. I might have been able to help if . . . well, I got separated from the truck. When the shit hit the fan, I was up at the intersection, and . . . anyway. Appreciate what you did here tonight."

"What I did here tonight was my job, Mr. Owens."

"Well . . . I just wanted to express my gratitude. I doubt I can make that sentiment public. . . . We, uh . . . have an adversarial relationship, after all. . . ."

"Only in your eyes, Mr. Owens."

Owens swallowed, vaguely embarrassed. "Well. At any rate. You may have saved some lives here tonight."

He offered his hand and Ness shook it; then the safety director helped Owens to the sound truck, which he drove slowly off.

"Interesting reaction," Curry said.

Ness grinned. "I'll be a villain again by tomorrow. And the Republic bigwigs aren't going to love me, either."

"Do you really care?" Bob Chamberlin asked.

"Not in the least," Ness said.

"Maybe we ought to put that labor-racketeering investigation on the back burner for a while," Chamberlin suggested. "Otherwise we risk looking anti-union, which is political suicide . . ."

"No way in hell," Ness said. "Bob, stay here and keep an eye on things. Albert, see if that sedan will still drive. I better get back to City Hall and make my report to the mayor . . . and get him to issue that proclamation I said he made."

3

"That's deuce," said Eliot Ness, in tennis whites, racket in hand, about to serve in the final set of a long game of doubles. Next to him was Mayor Burton, his sturdy frame leaning forward in anticipation of the return, and across the net from Burton was trim, bald, intense Frank Darby, president of the Chamber of Commerce and general manager of the May Company. Across the net from Ness was white-haired, wiry Cyril Easton, richest financier in the city. Of the four men on this grass court at Lake Shore Country Club, only Ness wore short pants; and of the four men on this court, from which Lake Erie could be shimmeringly seen, only Ness was not in his early fifties.

Nonetheless, the match had been hard fought. Ness played tennis well, though he was better at badminton and handball; the latter sports were part of a daily ritual at Dewey Mitchell's Health Club, whereas this complimentary membership to classily suburban Bratenahl's Lake Shore Country Club, with its golf-green-like tennis courts, was something new. He'd played on hard clay in Chicago and was just getting used to the faster play of grass.

Cleveland's safety director was physically in top shape, but these three older men were every bit as fit as he was: all of them worked out on a daily basis (Burton with Ness at Dewey Mitchell's), and the retailer and financier played with single-minded stamina that thirty-four-year-old Ness could only envy. Under a hot afternoon sun Ness and

Burton had won the first set 6–2, lost the second 4–6, won the third 6–4, and lost the fourth 1–6.

And now Ness fired his fastest serve, and Darby's return flew out of bounds.

Burton smiled at Ness; Ness smiled back.

Ness served again, another fast one, but Darby was ready and lobbed it behind Burton, who scrambled back and managed a weak but sufficient backhand return, while Easton moved in for the kill with a slashing forehand cross-court.

Ness tore after it, lunging, catching a piece of it, tumbling to the grass, skidding, as the ball sailed over the net, whizzed down the baseline, and just caught the inside corner, for match point.

Minutes later, the four men were sitting at a white wooden table under a yellow-and-white umbrella on the terrace bar overlooking the courts, the lake providing a blue backdrop and gentle breeze. They had toweled off but their whites were moist with the game. They drank martinis.

"You play an interesting game, Mr. Ness," Easton said. He had a warm white smile and cold blue eyes. His face was deeply grooved, his features sharp; his flesh was a golden brown nearly as rich as he was.

"So do you, Mr. Easton," Ness said.

"Yours is a thoughtful, almost scientific approach," Easton said reflectively. "But you aren't afraid to take risks—to put yourself on the line."

"Or my wardrobe," Ness said wryly, gesturing to the stripe of green he'd added to his white short pants when he'd slid across the court going after that last point.

Mayor Burton sipped his martini. "It's nice to get away from the office for a few hours. I appreciate the invitation, gentlemen."

"So do I," Ness said, smiling, but behind the smile was apprehension. He knew that in some way this silver cloud had to have a gray lining. Tennis or not, this was a business meeting, a meeting called by one of the most important men in the city. In the state.

In the nation.

Cyril Easton had arrived in Cleveland from Canada with his Baptist minister father back in 1901; the intelligent teenager had favorably impressed one of the elder Easton's congregation in the Euclid Avenue Baptist church: a certain John D. Rockefeller. Under that wealthy wing, young Easton flourished, supervising and expanding Rockefeller's utilities interests; later, when Rockefeller associates formed a syndicate to send Easton on a Canadian utilities venture, only to pull out in the panic of '07, Easton found Canadian backers and began building a personal fortune.

By the late twenties Easton's utilities holdings rivaled Samuel Insull's; he controlled Goodyear Tire and Rubber, and merged and purchased his way into control of Republic Steel. He was said to be worth one hundred million in 1929.

Before the crash, that is—after which he was left with a mere one hundred grand. Unlike Samuel Insull, however, whose fall included disgrace and imprisonment, Easton had slowly but shrewdly built his investment banking firm into the front ranks of international investment speculators. Among his many successes was financing the giant Fisher Body works here, providing thousands of jobs for Clevelanders.

While he no longer controlled Republic Steel, Easton remained on the board of directors. Which meant that the shadow of the Corrigan-McKinney strike fell across this white table on this sunny day.

No less significant was the presence of Frank Darby, who'd been general manager of the May Company since 1905, after making a success of the store's first shoe department. It had been Darby who convinced David May to live up to the company slogan "Watch Us Grow" by constructing a $2.5 million facility. That eight-story structure seemed less imposing today, in 1937, but the May Company, with its many locations nationwide, was flourishing even in this depression.

"I understand things are quiet out at Corrigan-McKinney today," Darby said.

"Knock on wood," Ness said. He had a drink of the cool martini. Sailboats dotted the lake, swaying lazily.

"You were in a difficult position," Darby said. "I for one think you handled yourself well."

"Neither the unions nor Republic had kind words for me in the press," Ness said. "But I can live with that."

Easton smiled thinly. "That's an interesting political view."

Burton laughed shortly. "I'm afraid none of Eliot's views are particularly political."

"Do you agree with his approach?" Easton asked the mayor.

The mayor hesitated, but his answer was what Ness had hoped it would be: "Yes. It's not the city's job to take sides in these matters. My director of public safety has taken steps to preserve the safety of the public—the very definition of his job."

Easton swirled his martini, the olive in which stared up at Easton like a single green-and-red eye. "There are those who think Mr. Ness takes too soft a position where the labor problem is concerned. There are those who feel that strikes are criminal activities and should be handled accordingly."

"Mr. Easton," Ness said softly, but with an edge, "the law of the land backs the rights of these workers to organize, and to go on strike."

"The New Deal," Easton said, with a faint tone of derision. "Unmitigated, unconstitutional horseshit."

"Perhaps," Ness said. "But as of now, collective bargaining is something that Republic Steel and industry in general are going to have to live with. And company goons, hired to beat, maim, and kill strikers, are engaging in some 'unmitigated, unconstitutional horseshit' themselves, wouldn't you say, sir?"

Easton smiled briefly, plucked the olive from the drink and popped it in his mouth. He chewed, swallowed, and said, "Mr. Ness, you do have a point. And this 'peace zone' you've established has unquestionably cooled the situation down. It's just that . . . well. There are those who think a firmer hand would have a longer lasting effect."

Burton winced.

"Mr. Easton," Ness said, "with all due respect, those who were shot down in the Memorial Day Massacre and at Massillon are enjoying the lasting effect of being dead."

Easton's face was a humorless mask. "Mr. Ness, communism is a serious problem. It's not a problem a man in your chair ought ignore."

Ness sat up straight. "Mr. Easton, the first thing a company like yours does when organized labor rears its head is brand any and all strikes, any and all unions, a communist plot. Next, they fund armed vigilante and citizens' committees as part of 'back-to-work' movements to break strikes."

Easton was frowning; Burton fidgeting; Darby listening.

"I won't be manipulated or intimidated or paid off into using my department as a goon squad for some steel company. Nor will I be shamed by unions into being their bodyguards."

"Eliot," Darby said, gesturing with an open hand, "I sympathize with your views, but the reality is that individuals in this city who have supported Mayor Burton—and have supported you—expect certain considerations."

Burton winced again.

"They won't get them," Ness said flatly. "I'm prepared to turn over the key to my boathouse, and resign from both country clubs where I've been given memberships, and resign from the various associations, and—"

"Eliot," Burton said, putting a hand on Ness's arm. "Please. No one is suggesting anything untoward here."

Easton motioned to a waiter for another martini and said, "Hal is right, Mr. Ness. I'm merely passing certain sentiments along to you . . . for your information. For your consideration. Your well-known conscience and integrity I would never compromise. They're your stock-in-trade, after all."

The sarcasm of that, gentle and lingering as the

breeze off the lake, was not lost on Ness. But he said nothing. He drank his martini; ordered another.

"I felt you should be aware," Easton said, "that there are those who feel that the strikers are keeping the plant closed via violence and intimidation . . . and, perhaps, violence in retaliation is the only logical response. For the good of the community."

Clouds were sliding across the sun; the afternoon was suddenly darker, cooler, at least for the moment.

Ness shook his head wearily and said, "Mr. Easton. Sir. Provoking violence—escalating the violence that's already there—will not scare the workers into line. In reality, every beating administered in the name of the company wins converts to unionism. You can get a great education from a nightstick or tear gas."

"Frankly, Mr. Ness," Easton said sadly, "I'm surprised to find you taking the side of the unionists."

"That's just it: I'm not taking their side. Or yours."

"What side are you taking, then?"

"Cleveland's."

Darby smiled tentatively. "Cyril—I don't think that's such a bad side for the Director of Public Safety to take."

Easton toasted Ness with a martini glass. "Match point, Mr. Ness."

"Eliot," Darby said, "speaking for the Chamber of Commerce, we aren't interested in seeing the Department of Public Safety used as a vehicle for 'union-busting.'"

"Nor am I," Easton said, not entirely convincingly.

"But," Darby went on, "we do expect you to pursue *criminal* labor activity."

Easton nodded vigorously. "There are gangster-dominated unions operating in this city that demand your attention."

"We refer specifically," Darby said, "to the situation as regards the glass workers and carpenters."

Ness shrugged and nodded. "Caldwell and McFate," he said.

James "Big Jim" Caldwell, vice-president of the Carpenters District Council and bargaining agent for the

Glass Workers Union, and James "Little Jim" McFate, president of the Builders District Council, held sway over thousands of Cleveland laborers.

"Those two are racketeers, plain and simple," Ness said. "No question of that, gentleman. No argument from me on that point."

"Anyone wishing to build in Cleveland," Darby said, leaning over, speaking in hushed tones, "has to pay tribute to those two racketeers, as you accurately describe them. It's extortion; a protection racket like something out of . . . out of . . ."

"Chicago," Ness offered, with a smile.

"Exactly," Darby said.

Easton leaned forward, his eyes tightening. "I'm concerned about these small-time hoodlums for one reason: they are costing our city dearly. We are the sixth largest city in these United States, Mr. Ness . . . but we're ranked *sixtieth* in building starts."

"The word has spread, nationwide," said Darby. "Cleveland is too expensive a place to build—in terms of the blackmail these 'union' representatives will inevitably demand."

Burton lifted an eyebrow and said, "Several major chain stores, in just the last six months, have abandoned plans to build here."

"Scared off," Darby said glumly, shaking his head. "And not just because of the money involved. These are violent men. Gangsters."

"Gentlemen," Ness said. "None of this is news to me. . . ."

"Then why," Easton asked tersely, "haven't you done anything about it?"

Ness looked at the financier coldly, saying, "I have been in office roughly a year and a half. During that time I have been engaged, primarily, in launching and personally supervising perhaps the largest investigation into police corruption in the history of this country. The number of successful prosecutions my office has—"

"My apologies," Easton said, raising a hand. "Your

record is nothing if not impressive. And, too, I know you've been engaged, of late, in investigating these awful 'butcher' slayings."

Ness nodded and said, "The so-called Mad Butcher of Kingsbury Run is thought by some to be dead, and by others merely to be . . . on hiatus. But I've been instructed, by Mayor Burton, to put my energies elsewhere. Right now, gentlemen, you should be relieved to know, I'm directing an undercover investigation into a labor racketeering case, which we're on the brink of cracking."

"Good," Darby said, pleased. "Good." The sun was out again, reflecting off Darby's pink skull.

Ness took a sip of martini, casually. "And our next target will be Big Jim and Little Jim. I can promise you that."

Easton smiled and nodded. "Very good." He, too, seemed pleased; placated, even.

"But I must tell you," Ness said firmly, looking directly at the Chamber of Commerce president, "that until one of your own steps forward to testify against Caldwell and McFate, I'm fighting an uphill battle."

Darby's eyes narrowed; part of it was the sun, part of it wasn't. "Eliot, these men are unscrupulous . . . they're dangerous."

"Yes they are. But you can't ask me to stop them, on the one hand, while on the other continuing to give into their various shakedown demands for the sake of expedience."

"That's not fair," Darby said. "The May Company has never—"

"I didn't mean you specificially, Frank. But the vicitimized members of the Chamber who are complaining to you, privately, need to complain to me, publicly."

Darby was sobered by that; he nodded, saying, "I'll see what I can do."

"I realize what I'm asking," Ness said. "Both Caldwell and McFate are entrenched in the community. Hell, Caldwell lives right here in Bratenahl! Moved to an expensive house out here couple years back. He's a neighbor of the very people he's exploiting. Some of them accept him as a necessary evil. He's a friendly enough fellow, when he isn't threatening you or busting up you or your property."

"He is at that," Darby said, with quiet frustration.

"I understand your problem," Ness said. "Behind the smiles and hail-fellows-well-met, these men are thugs, no doubt of it. They use violent vandalism as their lever."

"The sound of breaking glass," said Easton dryly, "has become a common one in this city."

"And when glass breaks," the mayor said, just as dryly, "it has to be replaced."

Which was where Big Jim Caldwell's Glass Workers Union came in.

"In the past eighteen months, gentlemen," Ness said darkly, "ten thousand plate-glass windows in Cleveland have been shattered—some by bricks . . . others by gunfire."

Leaving them with that statistic to ponder, Ness rose, declining another martini. He had work to do. An undercover investigation to look after. The McKinney-Corrigan stalemate to check up on.

Burton seemed relieved the meeting was over. Darby seemed pleased with Ness's anti-labor rackets pledge. Easton, Ness couldn't read. Shaking hands all around, racket tucked under his arm, Ness headed across the terrace lawn for the dressing room. As he did, he made note of another Lake Shore club member.

Sitting at a table, playing cards with several local businessmen, was a stocky, jovial man wearing a pastel yellow sport shirt and a smug expression.

Laying his cards down, the smug, jovial man said, "Gin."

And the others threw their cards in, smiling, shaking their heads, muttering about what a lucky bastard their friend was.

Like Eliot Ness, Big Jim Caldwell had won a game this afternoon.

4

Harry Gibson arrived at work a little drunk.

But then Harry Gibson almost always arrived at work at least a little drunk, a condition that no one ever commented upon, and which some, perhaps, failed to discern. After all, few of the merchants, farmers, or truckers who frequented the Northern Ohio Food Terminal had ever encountered Gibson in any other condition. To them, he was never less than a swaggering, towering son of a bitch. That he had booze on his breath was just another detail, not necessarily telling.

Gibson was a massive six foot two, a bruiser with brown slicked-back hair and a flushed face and lumpy but deceptively pleasant features that were usually set in a smile. It was a smile that Gibson wore even as he demanded his various pieces of the action from the merchants in the market; a smile he wore when a whore took off her slip; a smile he wore when he was breaking a farmer's leg.

As for arriving at work half tanked, well, that wasn't his fault, was it? He had to show up at three A.M., didn't he, and what else was there to do till three in the goddamn morning but sit in a saloon and soak up some suds? Six days a week he worked the market from before dawn till late afternoon, when he headed back for his flop, hit the hay, and crawled out again around nine at night to find a bite, a broad, a bottle, starting the cycle anew. It was a full life.

The Northern Ohio Food Terminal, at East Fortieth,

south of Woodland Avenue, was within a mile and a half of
the rough-and-tumble East Side neighborhood where Gibson
grew up. His pop, of whom Harry was said to be the
spitting image, had been a coke shoveler at a steel mill in
the Flats; at age forty-five the elder Gibson, his lungs
shot after breathing in God knew how much coal dust,
collapsed at work, losing his job, leaving the family responsibility to his three boys. Harry, the youngest, had
done his share, and still did help out the old man and old
lady. But he'd decided early on that such a life was not for
him; the steel mills, the factories, could do without Harry
Gibson. Blessed with his pop's brawn, Harry, who was
now thirty, had run with a street gang as a kid, got into
bootlegging as an older kid, and graduated into being a
union slugger, getting in tight with McFate and Caldwell,
who had a lock on the construction unions.

Harry knew that he probably could have turned an
even tidier buck if he'd followed some of his bootlegging
pals into the mob. But that was risky work—you could
wind up dead in a ditch, like with these policy-racket wars
that had been flaring up lately; or in stir, playing fall guy
for the big boys in the Mayfield Road gang, who made
sure *they* never did any hard time.

Besides, union work was something a guy like Harry
Gibson could be proud of. Helping the little guy not get
took advantage of, like his pop had been.

Harry was chairman (a title Big Jim Caldwell suggested)
of the Marketers Co-op Club; what this meant was vendors in the stalls inside and outside the sprawling food
market had to pay him weekly dues. If anybody failed to
pay, that's when Harry's negotiating skills were called into
play: stalls would be smashed, produce trashed, your
occasional arm or leg busted.

The service Harry provided the vendors, in addition
to making sure nobody gave any of 'em a bad time, was
being middleman between them and the farmers who
brought their crops to sell at the market. The Marketers
Co-op Club, which is to say Harry and his staff of twenty
strong-arm assistants, informed the farmers coming in

that they weren't allowed to unload their own trucks. Instead, they were required to hire two-man crews, handlers from the Drivers and Employees local, to do the work; it usually ran twenty-five bucks per small truck, fifty for a bigger rig. Any farmers or truckers who refused would again run into Harry's negotiating skills: tires slashed, vehicles wrecked, your occasional arm or leg busted.

There hadn't been much need for negotiation in the last couple weeks, not since Harry had sprayed one farmer's truck with machine-gun fire, lighting up the predawn morning like the Fourth of fuckin' July. It had been funnier than hell watching that farmer and his kid tuck their tails 'tween legs and go rattling out of the loading-dock area, barely able to steer that bullet-puckered hunk of junk out of the terminal. They were lucky it even drove.

Beyond his considerable negotiating skills, Harry, who was also the business agent of the Drivers and Employees local, could shut the market down with a snap of his thick fingers. With an item as perishable as produce, the union had the farmers and dealers by the balls; if Harry called a strike, forcing the handlers to quit work, the Northern Ohio Food Terminal would be a world of rotting goods.

The market, a big yellow-brick building, a block long and half again as wide, opened at five A.M.; but trucks began showing up shortly after three, jamming Fortieth Street, engines running, drivers waiting for the line ahead to move so they could pull up to the loading docks and empty their loads. It was a cool, clear morning, for now, though the sun would remind everybody it was July soon enough. Along the loading docks the unloaders in Harry's union stood in their leather aprons, waiting for the trucks to pull in; they looked bored, even though the air was filled with the shouts and honking horns of impatient truckers.

Soon the market would be crawling with buyers: men in business suits representing the chain stores; men without ties who were the smaller, local grocers, buying for their coming day, to fill the shopping lists not yet made

out by housewives around the city, who were sleeping now
but would be shopping later.

Some of the trucks were already being unloaded. One
of Harry's unloaders was up in the reefer, as the refrigerat-
ed trucks were called, swinging boxes of butter down to
another unloader, who was stacking them on the sidewalk,
six high, eight deep, like a small building. As Harry
passed by, his shoes crunched packing ice that had spilled
onto the sidewalk.

Harry liked working the market. He liked the hustle
and bustle. He liked the way the place smelled, even:
barrels of sauerkraut, sheep's milk cheese, candied ginger;
steam rising off the griddle of the hot-dog stand inside; the
scent of turnips and carrots as an unloader threw back a
tarp and hosed down piled bunches of greens. The place
was a second home to him: He'd done odd jobs here as a
kid; you could earn a few pennies and get some free
produce at day's end.

These days, in his exalted position, Harry never did
any physical labor, other than busting your occasional arm
or leg. He wore a shirt and tie under a leather jacket; his
khaki trousers were work pants, but rarely got dirty. He
walked along the aisle connecting the loading docks, enjoying
the sight of his union boys opening tailgates, untying
ropes, pulling tarps back, taking loads down. Putting
money in Harry's pocket. A relay team unloaded water-
melons from an open truck onto the dock and into the
market; crates of cantaloupes, sacks of potatoes, baskets of
tomatoes, were passed along and hauled into storage bins;
bunches of onions and turnips got stacked in a big green
mound, as green as money. As green as the money Harry
was making.

Now, just as the traffic jam out on Fortieth let up,
another was forming here along the loading-dock area.
Metal-wheeled dollies squealed as cooler boys trundled up
the wide ramp inside the terminal to the freight elevator,
next to which gigantic floor scales trembled under canta-
loupe crates. Unloaders maneuvered their two-wheeled
hand trucks, piled up with crates, around each other and

stacks of produce and a dozen other obstacles, swearing, yelling, but steering clear of Harry as he passed, their expressions momentarily tightening into smiles for their business agent, who found the noisy hubbub of the loading docks as reassuring as the ringing bell of a cash register.

Not all of them appreciated what he was doing for them, but that was okay with Harry. As long as they stayed in line. Long as they paid their dues.

Up ahead, two docks down, a small crowd had gathered; it had to be something good, Harry knew, to interrupt market activities in these bustling predawn hours. He walked in a straight line down the connecting aisle, causing unloaders operating hand carts to weave around him and out of his way, like motorists avoiding a child who has wandered onto a highway.

Two men—obviously farmers—stood at the rear of a modest, battered tractor-trailer rig, where they had just as obviously been stopped in the process of unloading crates of greens onto the dock. Two other men were confronting the farmers. These men wore leather jackets and shirts and ties, like Harry's; without ever suggesting it, Harry's goon squad (though neither he nor they thought of themselves as such) had adopted their leader's style of dress as a sort of uniform.

Jack Rose, a big black-haired boyo Harry had known since his kid gang days, was gesturing with a hand the size of a catcher's mitt.

"It's a buck an hour per man," he said in a raised voice, indicating he was repeating these words for perhaps the third or fourth time, "and it's a two-man job. And it's a good four hours' work."

"Four hours!" the older of the farmers said. A faintly freckled Swede, or maybe Norwegian, Harry figured; about thirty-five, thickly mustached, and pale for a farmer. He wore coveralls and a floppy straw hat. He was a hick if Harry ever saw one, and Harry saw plenty here at the market.

"My uncle told you, we can do it in under two hours ourselves," the other one said, a towheaded younger man, also in overalls but wearing a cap. He was pale, too, Harry noted, craning his neck to see better. License plate on their truck was New York.

"You don't understand," Rose said, smiling harshly. "It's union rules. You got to hire us. No choice in the matter."

"It's too much," said the mustached farmer, shaking his head no. "We can't afford it. We'll do it ourselves, thanks just the same."

Harry, staying in the second row of the small but steadily gathering crowd, decided not to get involved. Neither Rose nor the other man, O'Day, had spotted their boss looking on. It would be good to see how they fared in a confrontation. Two more of his boys, Callahan and Carney, in their leather jackets and shirts and ties, fell in next to their boss in the growing audience.

"I guess you never hauled into this market before," Rose was saying, in a slightly more friendly tone.

"Not in a couple of years," the mustached farmer admitted. "Now if you fellows would just go about your own business—"

Rose thumped the mustached farmer's chest with two stiff fingers. "This *is* our business. What are you, one of these smart guys? I got a good notion to pound you into this here pavement, pal. And we can tip over your truck, too, if you want, and if you ever come in here again, it'll cost you fifty fucking bucks to unload."

The two farmers looked at each other, shrugged, shook their heads no, and began unloading more crates onto the dock.

Jack Rose kicked one of the crates, splintering the wood.

The mustached farmer sighed, shook his head again, and calmly said, "That'll cost you, mister."

"No," Rose said, "it'll cost *you*."

He picked up another crate and smashed it on the cement, cracking it open, spilling out the contents, turning produce into garbage.

And now Rose and O'Day seemed aware of the crowd

around them, if not of Harry Gibson's presence in it, and that seemed to spur the pair on.

"Walk away now," the mustached farmer said, "or you'll have trouble."

"You *got* trouble," O'Day said, speaking for the first time, and he took a swing at the mustached farmer.

The farmer ducked out of the way, nimbly.

O'Day swung again, and his fist, his arm, cut the air like a saber, connecting with nothing, as the farmer slipped that punch as well.

Harry Gibson tapped Callahan on the shoulder and nodded at Carney, and the two men moved from the crowd to back up Rose and O'Day, who was swinging again. This time the farmer grabbed the arm as the punch swooshed by and swung O'Day like a square dance partner into the open tailgate of the truck and rocked the truck and its contents and O'Day and his contents. Struck hard at mid thigh by the tailgate, O'Day shrieked like a woman, shaming Harry, and the mustached farmer moved forward, grabbed O'Day by the shoulder and hand of his left arm and threw him onto the pavement with a motion not unlike a grave digger heaving a shovelful of dirt. O'Day landed in the spilled produce and did not get up, the greens making a wreath around his head.

Rose, stunned by this display, finally swung into action and managed to land a blow against the side of the mustached farmer's face, only something strange happened: the mustache flew off.

And so did the floppy straw hat, and the face of the farmer minus mustache and hat was all too familiar to Harry Gibson, who sucked air into his chest like a drowning man coming up for the third time.

Meanwhile, the tow-haired younger farmer was kicking Rose in the stomach, doubling the big man over, and when Carney moved in to help, the other farmer flipped him, with one of those goddamn Jap moves, landing Carney flat and hard on his back on the cement. The sight of that froze Callahan in his tracks and the younger farmer swung a hard sharp right hand that about took Callahan's jaw off at the hinges. When Callahan failed to go down, however, and came back for more, the younger farmer stepped inside Callahan's follow-up swing, grabbed his arm, turned his back on Callahan, and threw him over his shoulder.

And Harry Gibson's men were spread out on their backs, unconscious or otherwise out of commission, like kids making angels in the snow. Only the pavement wasn't snow, and Harry Gibson's men weren't angels.

Harry rushed into the terminal and went to a wall phone. He dropped in a nickel and called Caldwell at home.

"Holy Mary mother!" Caldwell said. "Do you have any idea what *time* it is, man?"

"I ain't calling to tell you what time it is," Harry said. "Other than it's later than you think. I'm calling to tell you that Eliot Ness and some kid just beat the ever-living shit out of four of my men."

"What? Are you drunk, you simple bastard?"

"They came in dressed like farmers and started unloading a truck. They baited my boys into a fight."

"And nobody recognized Eliot fucking Ness? I know your boys can't read, but they at least *see* the goddamn papers, don't they?"

Harry shrugged elaborately, made a face, as if Caldwell could see him. "He didn't look like himself. He had on this fake mustache and a floppy old hat. And I never seen this kid before who was with him, who is probably also a cop."

"Did you get in and mix it up yourself?"

"No."

A long sigh. "Well, that's one thing, anyway. Praise God for small favors."

"What should I do?"

"Don't trade any punches, for Christ's sake. But stand up for your union. Speak your mind."

"Which is what?"

A long silence. "Use your head, why don't you, Harry? For something other than raising a crop of hair."

"Are you coming down?"

"Are you crazy, or just stupid? It's not my union. It's your union. You're the business agent."

"But boss—you're the brains!"

"Well, the brains are going back to bed. Good luck to you, my boy."

The click in Harry's ear told him he was on his own.

A paddy wagon had arrived by the time Harry rejoined the crowd. His four leather-jacketed men were being handcuffed and escorted into the back of it by bluecoats. Several press photographers were shooting pictures of the event. How the hell, Harry wondered, did everybody get here so soon?

Ness, who had not put his hat or mustache back on, was speaking to the crowd that had, by this point, swelled to at least a hundred people. Among them were truck drivers, farmers, vendors, buyers—men, and a few women, representing every branch of life and business at the food terminal.

"This little impromptu performance this morning," Ness was saying in a mild, mellow voice, "is only one small part of an ongoing criminal investigation here at the terminal. My office has been aware, for some time, of the activities of a gang engaged in a shakedown racket here at the market, extorting money by threats and force. This gang of racketeers, operating under the guise of a labor union, has preyed upon you people long enough. And they have preyed upon the city of Cleveland long enough— driving up food prices, pushing buyers and sellers into other markets in other cities."

Harry's jaw tightened as heads around him were nodding as Ness's words hit home.

"Right now," Ness continued, "my investigators are working undercover in this terminal. They are gathering evidence but will, if necessary, abandon their 'cover' and intervene, if this so-called union's goon squad interferes with the daily operations of this market. Undercover officers will continue to work the terminal until these acts of violence and extortion end."

Many heads were nodding now, and even some scatterings of applause broke out. Harry Gibson's face was reddening; his teeth were clenched—his fists were, too.

"But to really clean up this market," Ness said, hands on the hips of his coveralls, "I need the cooperation of those of you who have been victimized. If enough witnesses come forward, we can shut down this phony union."

Gibson shouldered his way through the crowd. Standing up on the loading dock, he gazed coldly down at Ness.

"My name is Harry Gibson. I'm the business agent of what you're calling a phony union. We are, in fact"—he searched for the words, tried to remember things he'd heard Caldwell say—"a legitimate labor union organized and operated to protect the, uh . . . interests of our members."

From the crowd came the sound of a raspberry. Gibson glared back at blank faces.

"I know who you are, Mr. Gibson," Ness said evenly.

Gibson turned back to Ness and pointed down at him. "And I know who you are. You're a cop in the pocket of the moneyed class. You're a union-busting copper."

From behind the press photographers stepped a satanic scarecrow in a seersucker suit and straw fedora with a red band. He had a pad and pencil in his hands and a smartass look on his face.

"Sam Wild," the man said, looking up at Gibson, introducing himself. "*Plain Dealer.* What makes you think Mr. Ness is a union buster?"

"He was just down busting heads at the steel mill, wasn't he? Then he climbs up on that truck and plays God for the press. Look at him here, in his farmer getup." Gibson turned to the crowd. "This is just some lousy publicity stunt!"

"Not that lousy," Wild said, smiling, scribbling. He turned to Ness, who stood with arms folded near the younger cop/farmer (whose name, Harry later found out, was Albert Curry). "How about it, Mr. Safety Director? *Are* you against labor?"

"I'm against racketeers in labor," Ness said. His eyes traced the crowd. "I'm against racketeers in the police department." He shrugged. "I'm against racketeers."

And now applause rang out—not just scattered: widespread.

Harry Gibson, feeling naked as a head of lettuce, scowled, and pushed his way through the crowd, disappearing inside the market, feeling depressingly sober.

Outside, the sun was coming up.

5

Eliot Ness handed the report to County Prosecutor Cullitan, saying, "A little light reading for you, Frank."

Cullitan, standing behind his big oak desk in his first-floor office in the Criminal Courts Building, took the hefty black-foldered document and pretended to gauge its weight in one hand like a market melon he was considering.

"One hundred pages?" Cullitan asked, sitting, placing the report before him. The prosecutor was a large man, fifty-six years of age, his gray hair streaked by stubborn dark strands, his quiet manner belying the power that could erupt from him in a courtroom.

"Eighty-five pages," Ness said, shrugging, sitting across from the prosecutor. "But when you start taking the witness depositions, you'll need a bigger office to hold the transcripts."

"You got witnesses to come forward?"

"Over one hundred." Ness pointed at the black-jacketed report. "We've substantiated forty-five acts of vandalism, bribery, and extortion. The Marketer's Co-op has already been disbanded, and we've made twenty-one arrests."

Cullitan's smile was gently mocking. "That stunt of yours, at the food terminal last month, would seem to have paid off."

Ness smiled back, somewhat sheepishly. "Well, Frank—I don't like to think of it as a stunt exactly. . ."

Cullitan's smile settled in one cheek. "Even if your

reporter friend Sam Wild did happen to be on the scene, along with half the photographers in town."

Ness could only shrug.

Cullitan shrugged, too, his smile fading. "You took a chance, even so. This criticism you've been getting from both the AFL and CIO—you fueled it by following up your Republic Steel stint so quickly with this performance at the terminal."

Rather stiffly, Ness said, "I've taken chances before. If I only did my job when it was politically advantageous, then—"

Cullitan cut in: "I know you've taken chances. And I know your attitude toward politics. If I haven't made it clear, let me say that, uh, I'm grateful for what . . . well, I am grateful."

Both men lapsed into an embarrassed silence. What the prosecutor was referring to was this: the safety director, an appointee of a Republican mayor, had supported and campaigned for the reelection of a certain Democratic county prosecutor.

Ness shifted in the wooden chair. "This food terminal shakedown is only the iceberg's tip, Frank. Labor racketeering is just as widespread and entrenched in this town as police corruption was a year ago."

Cullitan smiled gently. "That just goes to show what can be accomplished in a year." He patted the report again, almost affectionately. "These witnesses wouldn't be coming forward unless they felt they could talk to the police without it getting back to the bad guys."

"I think we've built some trust," Ness said. "Particularly when my own staff is doing the questioning."

"You've assembled some good people. So . . . what's our next target? Caldwell and McFate?"

Ness nodded. "Caldwell and McFate."

"I take it you weren't able to tie them to the market shakedowns."

"No. Gibson is their man, but Gibson is not among those we've arrested."

"Why in hell not?"

"He—and his attorney—are taking the position that he is the bargaining agent for the union and was not aware that some of his members were 'overstepping their bounds.'"

"And his goons are backing him up, I suppose?"

"Yes. They're all taking his fall."

"That's an AFL union, isn't it?"

"Yes. And they're backing him . . . nominally. He has resigned from his post, and I understand a CIO union is attempting to organize the market."

"The Teamsters?"

"Yes."

"That's a rough bunch."

Ness shrugged. "Not for me to judge, unless they break the law. They're truckers, not interior decorators."

Cullitan's fleshy face was creased in a frown. "But that Teamster Whitehall, he's been a problem. . . ."

"He's a roughneck. We'll keep an eye on him. But in the meantime, Harry Gibson is out of work, anyway, if not in jail."

"Wasn't there *anyone* to testify against him?"

"No. Apparently his men did all the dirty work."

Cullitan's eyes narrowed. "Knowing Gibson's record, I find that difficult to believe."

"It's more likely the witnesses are simply afraid to finger him directly."

Cullitan rapped a fist on the report cover. "And he's the link to Caldwell and McFate."

"Yes. But I never held out hope this market investigation would lead us to them. We need to focus on the area where they are directly involved: building construction."

Cullitan raised his eyebrows. "Construction is hardly the word for it."

"*Destruction* is more like it," Ness agreed. He shook his head, smiled mirthlessly. "When I was studying criminology back at the University of Chicago, it never occurred to me I'd be chasing window smashers."

Cullitan laughed shortly. "Doesn't sound like a major crime, exactly, does it?"

"Not unless," Ness said, sighing, standing, "you're

talking ten thousand windows. I'll look forward to your reaction to my report."

And he shook hands with Cullitan and headed back to City Hall.

As Ness was nearing the private entry to his office, Sam Wild stepped out of the press room, just across the way. Wild wore his usual white seersucker suit and today's bow tie was blue.

"You turned your report in to Cullitan, I take it," Wild said, cigarette dangling from the corner of a sardonic smirk.

"Yes, Sam."

"Get any pictures taken?"

"No, Sam."

"You're losing your touch. You ain't had your picture on the front page in, what? Two weeks?"

"What's your point, Sam?"

"No point. Just giving you the needle."

"What's on your mind, Sam?"

Wild lifted his shoulders with studied casualness, set them down the same way. "I don't want to see you back off on this labor stuff, just 'cause some people are giving you a little heat."

"Why, is this an issue you care about?"

"The only issue I care about is any *Plain Dealer* with my by-line under a big juicy headline. Why do you think I got myself permanently assigned to the Ness beat? You're the best story in town."

"Why, thank you, Sam."

"What other safety director would go undercover just to make a bust himself? Corny, but effective."

"Corny?"

"Hey, I'm not being critical—if you hadn't made that bust yourself, the terminal shakedown wouldn't have got near the play in the press. Gotta hand it to you."

"I appreciate the kudos, Sam. Now, if you don't mind, I have a meeting—"

"You're going after Caldwell and McFate, aren't you?"

Ness said nothing.

"Off the record, of course," Wild said impatiently.

Ness said nothing.

Then he nodded.

Wild's eyes lit up like a hollowed-out pumpkin's on Halloween. "I want in."

"You'll be in."

"I mean, let me sit in on the meeting."

"I don't want any press coverage."

"I won't write it up. I just want in, on the ground floor of this thing."

"I don't think so."

"Come on! I've been a help in the past, haven't I? I can go places, do things, that your boys can't."

"Like break and enter, you mean."

"You said that, I didn't. Didn't you tell that one magazine interviewer I was your 'top unofficial investigator'?"

"That was in a weak moment. Over drinks."

"Don't be a dope! You want in-depth coverage on this one, don't you? Let me sit in."

Ness studied Wild's somewhat satanic yet earnest countenance, then said, "Okay. But keep your mouth shut, and don't write anything up till I give the okay."

"It's a deal."

Ness opened the door and went in and Wild followed.

Chamberlin, Curry, and Captain Savage were seated at one of the conference tables in Ness's spacious office. Savage, a short, rugged man in his mid-forties, headed up the Vandal Squad, which investigated bombings, window smashings, and other vandalism.

Standing near the window, smoking a cigar, was Will Garner, a beefy six-foot-four detective who had recently signed on with the safety director's office as an investigator. Garner was dark, his hair starkly black, though he was in his mid-fifties; he was a full-blooded Sioux, and had been one of Ness's "untouchables" back in Chicago.

"I've invited Sam Wild to sit in," Ness said.

Garner's frown was barely perceptible; Savage's you couldn't miss.

"Mr. Ness," Savage said, shifting in his chair, "I know

you and Wild are friends and all, and he's sympathetic to our cause ... but do you really think it's appropriate to have a reporter privy to our private planning sessions?"

Ness stood near the conference table. Wild stood off to one side, uncharacteristically mum, while Ness said, "We're facing a delicate situation. I don't have to tell you, Captain, of the perils of going up against a labor union, even if it is crooked. You've been painted a villain by every union in town, including the honest ones."

"Just because I try to do my goddamn job," Savage said resentfully.

"Right," Ness said. "Well, when the story of what we're trying to accomplish gets told, it will help that a sympathetic ear was listening right from day one."

Savage grimaced, but then nodded. Chamberlin and Curry, who were used to having Wild around, didn't react one way or the other.

"All in all," Ness said, "despite Gibson slipping through our fingers, the food-terminal operation has to be considered a solid success."

Curry was smiling. "I'll say. I got my picture in the paper."

"Dressed as a farmer," Chamberlin put in wryly.

The men smiled at that exchange, including Ness, who said, "And you all know what the next step is, or I should say *who* the next step is: Big Jim and Little Jim. Caldwell and McFate."

There were nods all around.

"For the record—I don't consider these men 'unionists.' To me, they're terrorists. They carry on immensely profitable rackets from inside the protective walls of organized labor. They have a hold that the rank-and-file union members can't break. But I think *we* can."

Ness sat at the conference table.

"Albert, you and Will have been doing some preliminary investigating. Fill us in, would you?"

Curry stood and said, "We've interviewed twenty-five potential witnesses—mostly building contractors. We've learned that the contractors are routinely forced to shell out fifty to three hundred bucks per job in construction blackmail."

"Either they make the payments," Garner said, "or Caldwell and McFate call a strike."

Savage said, "They do more than that: they vandalize the buildings under construction, ruin machinery, destroy supplies and materials—"

"And this is only what the contractors pay, up front," Garner said, relighting his cigar. Articulate as he was, his voice was slightly halting, and soft, but deep. "They are told not to tell their client about the shakedown; oh, they can pass the cost along to their client, naturally. But they aren't to say a word about it."

"Why?" Ness asked.

Garner's smile was like a fold in leather. "Because that way Caldwell and McFate can hit the owners up later, separately—using their glass scam."

"Glass is generally the last thing to be installed in a new building or a renovated one," Curry cut in. "And Caldwell and McFate don't approach the store owner until the eve of a building's completion."

"Which puts them in a vulnerable postion," Ness said, nodding, "having already invested a small fortune in a structure that has no windows."

"Exactly," Curry said. "And *won't* have any windows until the 'boys' are paid off."

Ness narrowed his eyes. "You say you've talked to the building contractors; have you gotten anywhere with their clients? The owners of the stores, of the businesses, that were victimized?"

"No," Garner said.

Curry was shaking his head no, as well. "They're still scared; nobody wants their store windows smashed, after all."

"And," Garner said, "we're still on an informal basis with the building contractors. We haven't turned any into grand-jury witnesses yet."

"I'm confident we can," Ness said. "We just have to let them know that there's safety in numbers."

"What do you mean, Mr. Ness?" Savage asked.

"We must assure our potential witnesses that none of them will be called to testify at any time unless there are twenty or thirty others like them who have agreed to do the same."

Again there were nods all around.

"Also," Ness said, "we'll promise—and give—police protection, whenever necessary. We'll put witnesses up in hotels or other 'safe houses,' if that's what it takes, under twenty-four-hour armed guard."

"Can we do that?" Curry asked.

"I think he means," Chamberlin said wryly, tiny mustache twitching, "can we *afford* it?"

"We have the mayor's full backing on this," Ness said. "Captain Savage, your Vandal Squad is assigned to my office for the duration of this investigation. You'll report directly to me, not the chief of the Detective Bureau."

"Yes, sir," Savage said.

"We're now, all of us, a special 'shakedown squad'—our primary focus to nail McFate and Caldwell. Now, Bob Chamberlin here will be in charge during my absences. Report to him, when necessary."

"Absences?" Curry asked; others were asking the same question with their expressions.

"I have a busy schedule of speaking engagements in the coming months," Ness said, "which will take me to Boston, Milwaukee, New York—"

"Speaking engagements?" Wild said, jaw dropping open.

"You're just an observer here, Mr. Wild," Ness said, with a gently scolding smile.

"Maybe so," Curry said, "but I'm as confused as he is."

"A lot of businesses have been chased out of town by these bastards," Ness said. "I may be able to round up some witnesses outside of Cleveland—big chain-store executives, for example—who will be willing to testify. But as far as greater Cleveland is concerned, I'm simply on the road, being its goodwill ambassador, making speeches, pressing the flesh. Understood, Mr. Wild?"

"Understood, Mr. Ness." The reporter was lighting up a Lucky.

Ness rose, leaned his hands on the table. "We need trial-proof evidence, gentlemen. If we're to give our witnesses real protection, we need to put Big Jim and Little Jim in a room where there's no danger of the windows being smashed—because in place of glass there will be steel bars."

6

Depression or not, Cleveland boasted one of the busiest, liveliest of American main streets: Euclid Avenue, where shoppers could stalk the big department stores— the May Company, Bailey Company, Halle Brothers, Higbee Company, and more. And so-called Playhouse Square, the concentration of theaters near upper Euclid from East Twelfth to East Eighteenth, offered theatergoers as impressive an array of entertainment as could be found this side of Chicago. Movie/vaudeville showplaces like B. F. Keith's Palace, Loew's State, and the Hippodrome, as well as the legitimate stage venues of the venerable Colonial Theater and the regal Hanna Theater, brought Broadway to the midwest, their glittering marquees lighting up the nights.

Right now it was afternoon, and the marquees were unlit, but the eyes of Big Jim Caldwell were electric and alive, as he and his partner, Little Jim McFate, strolled along Euclid. His eyes were fixed upon the restaurant across the street from the Hanna Theater, a restaurant whose plum position at the intersection where Fourteenth, Euclid, and Huron met, would be money in the bank for its owner, one Vernon Gordon.

And, of course, money in the bank for Big Jim Caldwell, as well—not to mention his partner Little Jim.

Jim Caldwell, his designation as "big" notwithstanding, was the smaller of the two men, both of whom (despite the August heat) wore off-the-rack but expensive, dark, vested suits and conservative ties; Caldwell wore a

57

derby, McFate a homburg. Stocky, genial, Caldwell was a round-faced man of forty-five years, his black hair receding at the temples, his small, dark, almond-shaped eyes magnified to a normal size by his thick-lensed, wire-frame glasses.

His companion, Jim McFate, was a lanky man a head and a half taller than Caldwell, with a long face, his eyes hooded and icy blue, his lips thin and frequently thinly smiling. A mild vein-shot reddening of the noses indicated both men drank too much, but only McFate ever drank during working hours. It had been a joke friends had inflicted upon them some time ago—calling the short, chubby Caldwell "big" and the tall, skinny McFate "little" —but good living had put pounds on Little Jim, and his paunch rivaled his partner's.

They had been together for just over five years. A West Side working-class stiff, McFate had gone from house painter to organizer for the painters union to business agent of that and several other unions—everything from barbers to bricklayers. His interests and those of Caldwell, with his positions with the glass workers and carpenters unions, soon converged. McFate had actually tried to shake Caldwell down, which had so amused the latter that he not only threw in with McFate, he put in the good word with Mo Horvitz and got Little Jim elected president of the Builders District Council, one of the city's most powerful building-trade locals.

Though the self-acknowledged "brains" of the team, Caldwell was actually newer to unionism that McFate. An East Sider who came up through kid gangs, Caldwell had done well for himself as pickpocket, till he got busted in '15; after he got out, he did some free-lance strong-arm work for the wops on Mayfield Road, until he got the idea for some shakedown rackets of his own. He was hitting dry-cleaning plants and cleaning up, till he shook one down that turned out to have Mo Horvitz as a silent partner. The Jews and micks were the real powers of the Cleveland crime syndicate, and Horvitz was Cleveland's Capone; but Caldwell's ties to the Italian, Mayfield Road branch of the syndicate at least kept him from winding up in a suburban ditch.

In fact, it was Horvitz who had encouraged Caldwell to move his talents into the union field, even opening a few doors for him, particularly with the Building Service Employees union.

Big Jim Caldwell had been in the union racket—and on easy street—ever since.

Now, as he and McFate approached the brick, two-story, corner restaurant, whose GORDON's sign consisted of a multitude of small moving white lights like those on many a Playhouse Square marquee, Caldwell paused to savor the sight of the row of boarded-up places where windows would be installed.

"Bucko," Caldwell said to his friend and partner, spreading his arms as if before a graven image, "we are about to partake of a feast."

McFate frowned. "Place ain't even open yet, laddie. I doubt you can get served."

Folding his arms, the smaller man said, "Oh, I'll get served. You'll get served. We'll both get served. Royally." And he smiled at his friend and his friend smiled back, finally getting the drift.

The front double doors were propped open, to allow workers easy entry and exit, and to help air the place out. Caldwell went on in, McFate bringing up the rear; heat and humidity immediately assaulted them. The moisture in the air was due to the plastering that was in progress: plasterers in white coveralls, shirts, and hats were busy along one wall, with their hawks and trowels, while across the wide room carpenters were nailing up lath along another wall, in preparation for the plasterers. The woodwork, unfinished, was already in; so were the booths, though they lacked the leather seats and backs that would be dropped in. Though the floor was bare but for sawdust, though no tables or chairs were in place, though not even a cash register was in sight, this dining room was almost complete. In little more than a week it would be open for business. People would be eating here.

That is, Big Jim Caldwell knew, they would be if Vernon Gordon played it smart.

Right now Vernon Gordon was standing in rolled-up shirt-sleeves, his tie loose, his brown pants plaster-smudged, hands on hips, surveying the work in progress with a tight, businesslike smile. An average-looking, brown-haired man of thirty-two with a sharp-featured, intelligent face, he might have been another worker. At best, a foreman. He was not: he was the boss; the owner, or at least one of them.

Caldwell was well aware that the success of the Gordon's restaurant chain was due to Vernon Gordon's business sense and hard work. Gordon had gotten out of business college in '24 and expanded his farmer father's modestly successful buttermilk stand in the Old Arcade by adding a lunchroom on Eighth Street, then a restaurant in the Citizen's Building, and gradually facilities in Detroit, Pittsburgh, and New York. Caldwell knew very well that Gordon was smart and shrewd, all right. But that didn't mean that he would be any less vulnerable to Caldwell's pressure.

"Hard to believe folks will be dining in this damp, dusty hellhole," Caldwell said pleasantly, "just days from now."

Turning at the sound of Caldwell's well-modulated voice, Gordon noticed the two men for the first time; the faintest grimace, which he suppressed, tipped his true feelings.

But he said, as pleasantly as Caldwell, "Good afternoon, gents. Yes, it's hard to believe how close to feeding the public we are at this stage . . . but we will tidy up a bit first. We'll begin painting tomorrow. Then the glass goes in, the light fixtures and, well . . . all the trimmings."

"Have to give you credit," Caldwell said, tucking his gripped hands at the small of his back, rocking on his heels, "for being one savvy businessman. Figuring that the common folks, who can't afford the Bronze Room, need a nice place to stop by after the show for a bite." He whistled. "I guess landing this corner doesn't come cheap."

Gordon's smile was as momentary as a twitch. He said, "No it doesn't. I don't find much comes cheap when it comes to renovation."

From behind Caldwell the solemn McFate nodded and said, "Wise words."

"It'd be a pity, wouldn't it?" Caldwell said abruptly.

"What would?" Gordon asked.

"If you couldn't open."

Gordon bit off the words: "And why would that be?"

"You're leasing these premises, aren't you?"

"I own this business, but I am leasing the property, yes."

"At a rate of fifteen hundred dollars a month, I believe."

Gordon said nothing; his eyes narrowed to slits.

McFate made a clicking sound in his cheek; his expression was mournful. "One hundred and twenty-five thousand dollars remodeling expenses, we hear."

Irritably, Gordon said, "More like one hundred and fifty. My contractors use strictly union labor, as you boys well know."

Caldwell sighed. He pointed over to a corner of the room where the wall was nailed with lath, ready for the plasterers; but at the moment it was deserted, but for an empty mortar boat waiting to be filled with horsehair-laced plaster.

"Step over to my office, Mr. Gordon," Caldwell said.

And without waiting, Caldwell walked over to that quiet corner, with McFate following dutifully. Gordon paused, rooted in the spot, clenching and unclenching his hands, his jaw.

Then he sighed heavily and joined the two men.

The background sound of work, the hammering in particular, kept their conversation private. Gordon's expression was one of anger mixed with fatigue; McFate had the dour look of a hanging judge, while Caldwell remained as cheery as a department-store Santa.

"We're calling the painters and glaziers off the job tomorrow," Caldwell said. Ho ho ho.

Gordon's eyes showed the white all around. "You're *what?*"

"I believe you heard me."

"Why? I've met all the requirements of your various goddamn unions . . . I pay on time, I—"

"I'm glad to hear that."

"What?"

"That you pay on time. Because it's going to cost you two thousand dollars."

"For what in hell?"

"For us to tell our people to go back on the job. You see, my friend Mr. McFate here and I may have to step in to settle a jurisdictional dispute amongst several of the unions involved in this renovation of yours."

"This is outright extortion."

"It's business, Mr. Gordon. You know all about business. You're one of the up-and-coming young businessmen in this city, after all. In this nation. Do the right thing, Mr. Gordon. Do what's right for business."

"I'll go to the police. I'll go to Ness."

"You'll go there without windows. You'll go there with unpainted walls. This conversation, by the by, is one we haven't had. Neither my partner here nor I will have any memory of it. What we will have is a list of grievances longer than an elephant's dick, and we'll call a strike and you won't be able to do anything except sit in here and look at your unpainted walls, your unfinished woodwork, and these unsightly boards blocking the lovely view of Playhouse Square designed for all the customers you won't be able to seat."

Gordon's face was as white as the plasterers' coveralls. Whiter. He pointed to the door like a merciless father sending his fallen daughter away. His voice was trembling with rage. "Get. Out."

"Talk to your business partners. I'll need a decision by"—Caldwell withdrew his pocket watch from his vest and made a show of studying it—"eight tonight. I'll be back personally for your decision."

Almost yelling, Gordon said, "Get the hell out! Both of you!"

At this, the hammering stopped; the plasterers in their whites and the carpenters in their coveralls looked at the two union reps who were leaving, smiling and waving at the men as they went, like politicians on parade. Several of the workers grinned and waved back. Others had looks of disgust and did not.

By eight that evening, however, the interior of the unfinished Gordon's restaurant was empty, but for Vernon Gordon and Big Jim Caldwell.

Gordon, wearing a suit and tie now, stood in the midst of the big empty room like an actor about to do a monologue on a stage. Outside, the myriad moving lights of marquees were making a glowing Great White Way of Playhouse Square; but the GORDON's sign was not yet lit, and the interior was barely lighted by a single jury-rigged hanging bulb. The unfinished dining room, sawdust and plaster stains on the uncarpeted floor, was shadowy and cool, now, the heat and humidity having left with the workers and the daylight.

It was a weary, resigned Gordon who said to Big Jim Caldwell, who had come alone, "I've talked to the other officers of my company. The consensus—with which I don't agree, not that it would matter to you—is that we should consider this a business expense, and pay."

"I think that's a wise decision," Caldwell said brightly.

Gordon cocked his head. "But business expenses need to be reasonable."

"Reasonable. And what do you and your officers consider reasonable?"

"Five hundred dollars."

Caldwell's affable mask dropped and he spat out the words. "No way in fucking hell. Two thousand or be damned!"

Gordon was taken aback, as if a furnace door had opened and flames reached out for him. Swallowing he said, "Six hundred, then."

"No. Not enough. Two thousand. I got to have two thousand."

"That's unreasonable."

Caldwell thumped the restaurateur's chest with a stubby finger. "Maybe you could put up a new sign: Gordon's Open Air Café. 'cause without windows, my friend, that is what you'll have."

Impulsively, Gordon blurted, "One thousand, damn it. I can't go a nickel higher."

"For two thousand," Caldwell said smoothly, "I'll see to it you get nothing but the best. Not just plate glass, but bulletproof glass."

"No. One thousand is my top offer."

"Two thousand."

"Be reasonable, man!"

"Two thousand."

Gordon stood shaking his head, thinking. Then, through his teeth, he said, "I want to open. I want to open my goddamn restaurant up. We'll go fifteen hundred. I'm not authorized by my officers to go that high, but I'll go back to them, if you agree to take it, and ask them to authorize it."

Caldwell considered that. "And if they don't authorize it?"

Gordon spat out his response: "I'll kick in the extra five hundred, out of my own pocket."

Caldwell began to smile. He rocked on his heels. "Well. Compromise is the better part of valor, they say."

Gordon said nothing, but anxiety was flickering in his eyes.

"All right," Caldwell said. "We'll settle on fifteen hundred. But the glass installed is going to be standard plate glass, not bulletproof."

"Fine, fine, fine. Whatever you say."

"As far as payment goes, we'll need it in cash, of course."

"Do you want me to deliver it to you, at the union hall?"

"No! I'll have my associate Mr. McFate stop by. You'll go for a ride in his Lincoln sedan."

Gordon laughed shortly. "I've *already* been taken for a ride."

Caldwell raised a scolding finger and said, "Tut tut, now. Let's not be bitter. It's just a matter of business, after all. By the way—once you have your windows installed, you're going to need somebody to wash them."

"Well . . . I suppose so. But I have people on my staff who—"

"Here's a reliable union firm," Caldwell said, handing him a card.

Resignedly, Gordon took the card and slipped it in a suitcoat pocket.

"Of course I'll need to run some interference for you, with the window washers union."

"What?"

"One hundred dollars a month. Small price to pay for the knowledge that your windows will be clean . . . and unbroken."

"I'm getting a little tired of your threats, Caldwell."

"Then I'd suggest you get some rest." He glanced about the now completely plastered room. "Getting a joint like this going is a big job. Big responsibility." He smiled at his victim. "You must be exhausted."

And he tipped his derby and left Gordon alone with his thoughts and his unfinished restaurant.

7

The neighborhood was working class, edging into lower middle class, a street lined with duplex houses marked by the overhang of second-story porches. They were built close together, simple wooden-frame houses, unlike the brick two-flats Ness was familiar with back in Chicago. But they were well-kept, freshly painted structures that indicated Jack Whitehall had, to some degree, "made it."

Ness left his black Ford sedan across the street, just down from a Sohio station and in front of a ma-and-pa grocery. The zoning in Cleveland was loose as hell; commercial and even industrial mixing in with residential like this was common, though it always threw Ness a little.

The night was dark—the blackness emphasized by a broken streetlight—and it was warm. But Ness was not sweating. He rarely did, even on a close night like this one.

Whitehall and family lived downstairs (Whitehall owned the duplex). Ness went up the short flight of wooden steps to the front porch, where he rang the bell.

An attractive dark-haired woman of about thirty, in a blue-and-white floral print dress and an apron, opened the door and smiled shyly, tentatively.

"Mr. Ness?" she asked through the screen door, arching her eyebrows. She had a sweet, almost melodic voice—feminine, rather timid.

"Yes." He removed his hat. "Mrs. Whitehall?"

66

"Yes," she said, with another shy smile, and opened the door. "Please come in."

Ness stepped in. There was no vestibule; he was immediately in a modestly but well-furnished living room. Other than Ness and Mrs. Whitehall, who took his hat, the room was unpopulated. Several windows were open and an electric fan was going. There was an overstuffed couch upholstered in green mohair, and a matching overstuffed chair with a standing lamp, turned on. Nearby was a coffee table where a sweating bottle of beer sat on a *Liberty* magazine next to a copy of the novel *Of Mice and Men*. A big console radio was softly playing orchestral music, a syrupy rendition of "Pennies from Heaven." On the wall were several framed prints, including one of sheep grazing on a hillside, and another of Jesus, a three-quarter front view of an almost feminine, cow-eyed Christ in soft sepia tones. The latter print was very familiar to Ness: he'd seen the original in a church in downtown Chicago, and framed prints in countless Chicago homes since. Never before in Cleveland, though.

"I'm just washing the dishes," Mrs. Whitehall said, with a quick smile and a nervous gesture toward the kitchen, a blur of white visible through an archway. "We eat in two shifts around here, you see. The girls eat around six, and I feed Jack around eight, or whenever he gets home."

Ness returned her smile, saying, "Goes with the territory." The hours from five in the afternoon till eight at night were key to a union organizer like Whitehall, who had to approach prospective members after they'd got off work.

"Jack will be with you in a moment," she said. "If you'll excuse me . . ."

"Certainly."

"Please make yourself comfortable," she said, gesturing to the overstuffed couch. He sat. She gave him one more quick smile and disappeared, with his hat in her hand, into the kitchen.

Ness got up and wandered about the living room. He

picked up a Shirley Temple doll from the floor and placed it gently on a table. He bent to examine the titles in a waist-high glass-and-wood bookcase along one wall; the authors ranged from Lenin and Trotsky to Edna Ferber and Sinclair Lewis.

The slightly muffled sound of a flushing toilet signaled the imminent arrival of the man of the house. Ness wandered back toward the couch but did not sit. When Jack Whitehall entered the living room, all six foot four and two hundred pounds of him, he gave Ness a stern look, but Ness smiled pleasantly at him and Whitehall suddenly laughed.

"You bastard," Whitehall said, not without affection. "You got your nerve. Sit the hell down."

Ness sat the hell down.

So did Whitehall, in the overstuffed chair. Dark-haired, white-complected Whitehall, his white shirt-sleeves rolled up, sweat stains under his arms, looked every bit the roughneck he was reputed to be in local union circles; jaw like a shovel, nose lumpy from innumerable breaks, ears cauliflowered, eyes lidded, he looked like a brute. But under the sleepy, sullen hoods of his eyes, something glittered. Something alert. Something intelligent.

"It was your idea, Jack, to meet at your home."

He had a drink of his beer. He didn't ask Ness if he wanted one. He didn't offer a hand to be shaked. He only offered the following pronouncement: "I'm not going to go sneaking around to see you, Ness. People would get the wrong idea. You come to my house, you're just a cop giving an honest union guy a bad time."

"I'm not here to give you a bad time, Jack."

Whitehall's scowl returned; he gestured menacingly with a massive, callused hand. "You sure as hell gave the union a bad time at Republic Steel. You don't have much of a memory, for a guy that worked a factory job."

"I did the union a favor at Republic Steel. They're at the bargaining table now."

Whitehall slammed the beer bottle down on the *Liberty* magazine. "Bullshit. I see the papers. I see the society columns. You're thick with those high-hat bastards. With those"—Whitehall seemed about to utter something truly distasteful—"captains of industry."

"I hold a high public office, Jack. I have to deal with all sorts of people in my line of work."

Whitehall sneered, gestured to himself archly. "Even low-life types like me?"

Ness glanced around the room. "I'd say you're doing pretty well. I'd say you haven't worked a factory job yourself in some while."

Whitehall bristled. "Maybe not. But I'm a good goddamn closer to what the man on the line is thinking and feeling and wanting than some half-assed, so-called public ser—"

"Jack. Don't look for an argument where there isn't one."

"Look, Ness—"

"It used to be Eliot—or 'kid.' Has it been *that* long?"

Whitehall tried to maintain his scowl, but it dropped away like the mask it partially was, and he grinned, and shook his head. "I guess maybe it has been."

Fifteen years ago, back in Chicago, Whitehall and Ness had worked together at the Pullman plant; Whitehall, a few years older than Ness, working class through and through, had been preaching communism and unionism even then. Ness, son of a small businessman, had no interest in unions, felt that a guy could better himself if he worked hard, if he excelled.

"I always liked you, Eliot," Whitehall said, his tone warmer now. "But you were full of shit even then. All you could think about was how to get ahead. You never stopped to ask yourself: How can we make things better for everybody?"

"I put myself in charge of me, Jack, and everybody else in charge of themselves."

"You think it's that simple, huh?"

"Pretty much."

Whitehall shook his head, heaved a sigh. "Well, it

worked for you, all right. You ended up in the front office, and then before long you were off to college. And now look at you. Young man on the move. On his way up. What's next? Mayor?"

Ness shook his head no. "I like being a cop, Jack."

Whitehall smirked. "You would."

"It's a profession like any other."

"Not hardly. Why did you pick it, Eliot?"

Ness shrugged. "It seemed wide open to me. Most of my peers were going into the business world. Law enforcement seemed backward. A field just waiting for somebody to take a more modern approach."

"You saw an opening and you took it."

"That's right."

Whitehall sighed again, wearily. "A leader like you, it's a goddamn shame. We could've used you."

"I don't like being used."

"Tell that to your pals at the country club."

"You really do want to argue, don't you, Jack?"

"We just don't see eye to eye on things, Eliot."

"I'm not against your cause, Jack. I just don't choose to make it mine. But I did help you recently. That much you have to grant me."

Whitehall smiled slowly. The hooded eyes seemed amused, and warmer. "The food terminal, you mean."

"Yes. We've gotten rid of Gibson and his goons. That leaves the door wide open for you and your Teamsters."

He was nodding. "Yeah, it does. And we'll walk right in."

"You see an opening and you'll take it. So say thank you, Jack."

"Thank you, Eliot."

"I'll be damned if you don't sound like you mean it."

"I'll be damned if I don't. But you didn't ask for this meeting to talk about the food terminal, did you?"

"Only to say that I expect the Teamsters to act like a real union at the terminal, and not a goon squad. If you do, we'll step right back in and shut you down quicker than you can say Harry Gibson."

Whitehall's eyes had turned cold again; he seemed offended. "We're not goddamn extortionists."

"No. But your strong-arm tactics are well-known. You've been up on a lot of charges, Jack."

Whitehall shrugged. "I'm up on one now."

"A serious one."

"A serious one. Assault to kill. A goddamn trumped-up charge and you know it."

"I don't think it's trumped up. I wish it were."

Whitehall and two of his cronies had been involved in a disturbance at a polling place during the last election. A uniformed cop had tried to break it up, and Whitehall had put the slug on the cop and taken his revolver away.

"You have a reputation for using strong-arm tactics, for being Cleveland labor's bad boy. You were a chief suspect in that coal-company office bombing. You did ninety days after you tipped over a furniture truck and beat up its driver."

Whitehall said nothing.

"I understand the Teamsters District Council president has put you on notice: you're to be on your good behavior from here on out, or you'll *be* out."

Whitehall blew air through his nose like an angry bull. "The rank and file will never let that happen. The day that assault-to-kill indictment was brought, my union guys unanimously reelected me secretary/treasurer of the local!"

"But I wonder what a jury will do?"

Whitehall winced at that and sat back in his chair.

"What," Ness said, casually, "if I could arrange to have that indictment dropped."

Whitehall gazed suspiciously at his one time co-worker. "Why would you do that, Eliot? Old times' sake?"

"I want your help."

"Help the cops? No way. No way in hell."

"Hear me out."

Whitehall cut the air with two crossing motions of his arms and hands, like an umpire calling Ness out at the plate. "I shouldn't even be talking to you. My union guys got no love for the cops, as you damn well know, and hell, you're worse than a cop. I wish you were just a cop, but you're a former G-man. Do you have any idea what your pal J. Edgar Hoover is trying to do to the unions of this country? The FBI is about the biggest union-busting operation there is!"

"I was never an FBI man, and Hoover is no 'pal' of mine."

"I don't care. You're an ex- G-man. You're no friend of mine."

"I'm no enemy, either. Do you view unionism as just another racket?"

"Hell no! Do you?"

"It can be."

"Well . . . of course it can be. So can the cop business, as you well the hell know."

Ness pointed a finger at him. "Right. And it took somebody like me, working on the inside of the department, to clean *up* the cop business."

Whitehall's eyes narrowed. "What are you saying?"

"We got rid of Gibson at the food terminal, but we couldn't get to his bosses—Caldwell and McFate. They were too well-insulated."

Whitehall's expression turned from hostile to thoughtful. "Those bastards are a cancer on the Cleveland union scene," he said, to himself more than Ness.

"Then help me cut 'em out."

Whitehall's expression was pained. "I'm not really in their camp, Eliot."

"You have *some* dealings with them. You're not on *bad* terms with them."

"No I'm not. Not really. I . . . I have to deal with them, from time to time. We have to swim in the same water, even if they do foul it."

Ness held up a cautionary palm. "All I'm asking is for you to keep your eyes and ears open. To pick up on any inside information you can."

"I'm not a goddamn informer!"

"This is Caldwell and McFate we're talking about,

Jack. The Tweedle-Dee and Tweedle-Dum who have almost single-handedly turned unionism into racketeering in this town."

"I'm not an informer."

"I need your help. The cause you believe in needs these two gone. And, beyond that, I can get that indictment against you dropped."

Whitehall thought that over. He got up and paced. From the kitchen came the clink of china as dishes were washed and dried. Kate Smith was bellowing "Whistle While You Work" over the radio, but the volume was way down.

Whitehall came over and stood before Ness and said, "What do I have to do, exactly?"

"As much as you feel you can."

"What if I don't find anything out?"

"I'm not a communist, Jack. I only reward those who excel."

"You're a smug, snotty little bastard these days."

"And you're a brutal son of a bitch who thinks the ends justify the means. Now that we've got that out of the way, do we have a deal?"

Whitehall snorted a laugh and said, "We have a deal."

They didn't shake on it. Whitehall just sat back down, but next to Ness on the couch this time, and said, "How much do you know about how Caldwell and McFate operate?"

"I know their general modus operandi," Ness said, and recapped the Caldwell/McFate approach of hitting up store owners on the eve of a building's completion.

"There's a hell of a lot more to it than that," Whitehall said.

"Oh?"

"Are you aware of the window washers union that Caldwell put together?"

Ness sat forward. "No."

"Well, the first round of bribes is just the beginning. If the store owner doesn't pay Caldwell a regular tribute— the amount varies from place to place, according to what the traffic will allow, I understand—the window smashing starts in again. And, of course, the blacklist kicks in."

Ness's brow knit. "Blacklist?"

Whitehall shrugged. "It's a list of window-smashing victims and victims-to-be. Merchants who will not be allowed to purchase glass in the city of Cleveland until they come to terms with Caldwell and his window washers union."

"When you say 'blacklist,' do you mean that in a literal sense?"

"What do you mean?"

Ness felt the excitement surge within him. "I mean, are we talking about a list of people that is more or less understood . . . or is there an actual, physical document?"

"It's a real list. There are probably several copies—circulated to the various glass companies in town, and agents of McFate and Caldwell, although I understand Big Jim and Little Jim make all their own initial contacts."

"Elaborate, please."

"Well, they handle most of their shakedown rackets personally—instead of being 'well-insulated' like they were at the food terminal, here they make sure that only themselves and their victims are witness to the initial demands, and the resulting payoffs. They carry out a lot of their own threats, too, I understand. They both did their share of strong-arm work, before they made it big."

"If a blacklist truly exists, it's a document that could convince any grand jury to indict those sons of bitches. . . ."

"So if I could get ahold of a copy of that list . . . ?"

"That assault-to-kill charge would disappear faster than Houdini."

Whitehall smiled thinly, studied Ness from those sharp, hooded eyes. "Are you blackmailing me, Eliot?"

"No," Ness said pleasantly. "I'm just providing you with an incentive. It's something we capitalists believe in."

With that Ness rose. Whitehall went into the kitchen and returned with Ness's hat.

Taking it, Ness said, "You have a lovely wife, Jack."

"I know. I got two great kids, too. Girls."

"I'd like to meet them."

Whitehall opened the door. "I don't know when you'll get the chance, 'cause we won't be meeting here again."

Ness tipped his hat. "But we will be meeting. Good night, Jack."

The men shook hands, finally, and Ness slipped out into the dark night.

8

Vernon Gordon sat in his restaurant, in a booth, in the dark, on the Thursday night before the facility's Friday opening. It was approaching midnight and Gordon was alone, the carpenters and painters and electricians gone, having finished their finishing touches, the lingering odor of paint and varnish the only remaining sign that the restaurant was not yet a going concern. Gordon sat in shirt-sleeves and loosened tie and paint-stained slacks, hands folded before him almost prayerfully, wearing a small, satisfied, but not quite smug smile.

It had all gone well. There had been minor hitches, primarily the petty shakedowns of Big Jim Caldwell and Little Jim McFate; but putting up a restaurant in a city of any size required a certain number of payoffs. Gordon expected that; it had been worse in New York and Detroit, actually. At least here in Cleveland—since Ness became public safety director, anyway—there was little graft on the city level. They hadn't even been approached for the usual building-inspector palm greasing. That made it almost a trade-off: less city graft, more union shakedowns. Business expenses. You had to learn to live with it.

Gordon sat and looked out the window at the glittering Playhouse Square night, streaked with neon, alive with moving marquees, slashed by automobile headlights, a sparkling darkness that blurred into something abstractly beautiful.

The street was hopping, but Gordon was not. He was

bone tired. He didn't mind, though; in fact, he liked it. He liked sitting alone in his new creation with its smell of newness, from the disinfectant of the kitchen to the leather of this booth; it was like sitting in a brand-new car you'd bought—and paid cash for.

He knew he'd been blessed—the only son of a successful farmer—but he also knew he'd never had it easy. His pop had made him work side by side with the hired hands, and, while he liked to work outside and didn't mind physical labor, he'd had no real affinity for farming. The business end of it had interested him, true, but he could not picture himself taking over the reins of the farm.

In 1922 Gordon, still in college (at Case Western, studying business), encouraged his father to cut out the middleman and open a buttermilk stand. The stand, a small, standup affair under a stairway in the Old Arcade, served as an outlet for the farm's daily products and for Ma's Dutch apple pies.

Two years later, when Gordon graduated, he was handed the buttermilk stand by his father to run as he saw fit; shortly thereafter, using profits from the unexpected killing the stand had made thus far, Gordon opened a second outlet. He picked up the lease on the stall for peanuts—the last tenant had gone out of business, running a tiny coffee shop within the office building; but Gordon punched out a door and window on Eighth, the narrow street across from the Hippodrome, a popular movie palace. He offered a limited menu (two sandwiches— toasted cheese and bacon-lettuce-and-tomato; and two varieties of pie—Dutch apple and lemon meringue) and kept the place open fourteen hours a day, to get the theater crowd and the usual luncheon set.

His father was proud of Gordon's success, but had no real interest in getting involved with the restaurants, other than as an outlet for his dairy farm's products; he completely gave Gordon his head. And in that head Gordon had an idea for a new kind of restaurant.

Good, simple food, served in nicely decorated but

not ritzy surroundings. Designed to suit the common man's taste (utilizing Ma's recipes) while at the same time making him—and his family—feel they were out for a night on the town. Gordon envisioned a chain of such restaurants, from the very start; if hamburger stands and automats could go national, why not this? Buying foods in bulk, various other supplies in quantity, uniform layout and design . . .

The Playhouse Square restaurant would take the place of the Eighth Street location, which had closed its doors that very day. The hole-in-the-wall lunchroom would be replaced by this study in mahogany paneling and clear crystal lighting. Flashier than the New York, Detroit, and Pittsburgh locations, this would truly be the highlight of the growing Gordon's chain. Which was fitting, as this was their Cleveland crown jewel, the Gordon family's home-base showcase.

Vernon Gordon did not remember falling asleep. He had been sitting in that booth, relaxing, reflecting, enjoying the smells of the new, savoring the exhaustion of this long final workday, knowing that his wife and two kids were already in bed asleep in their Shaker Heights home, that a few quiet moments here, alone, with his new pride and joy, wouldn't hurt a thing. Would, in fact, give him a good measure of simple pleasure.

But, at some point, he put his head on his folded arms and sleep sneaked up on him, subtly.

Less subtle was the gunfire that awoke him.

"Christ!" he yelled to nobody as glass shattered, and he ducked under the booth as it was showered with shards, while the thunder of machine-gun fire ate up the night and the plate-glass windows that looked out on the square.

He'd caught a glimpse, just a glimpse, out that shattered, shattering window, of the black snout of a machine gun sticking out the window of a black car stopped out in the street; a black snout spitting flame and smoke and .45 slugs.

And still they came, raking the restaurant, a lead rain

falling, making plaster clouds, splintering woodwork, knocking over chairs, tearing tablecloths, cutting grooves in counters and tabletops, puckering the metal of coffee urns and counter trim and cash register, tearing the leather of the booths, turning dishes, glasses, table settings, light fixtures to rubble, as the low-throated chattering of tommy-gun fire accompanied the dissonant music of breaking glass.

Gordon Vernon was no coward, but he cowered beneath the booth nonetheless, as any man would, while the table above him was served a noisy meal of glass and debris.

And when, finally, the gunfire stopped, all sound in the universe seemed to stop as well—other than the beating of Gordon's heart, which was pushing at his chest. Even with the havoc that had been visited upon the restaurant, no sounds broke the lull. Somewhere in his rattled mind Gordon noted that at least no water pipes had been burst, or he'd hear them spraying.

Then an angry squeal of tires announced the departure of the gunman—or gunmen, Gordon couldn't know—and he was alone with the wreckage that had been his restaurant.

And when he crawled out from under the tabletop, he did two things he hadn't done in a very long time: he screamed in pain, like a child who'd badly scraped both knees; and then, like that same child, he began to weep uncontrollably.

The tears weren't tears of pain, however, but of loss, and not monetary loss, not entirely. Something precious had been destroyed. Something Vernon Gordon had made, something he took pride in, something he had come to love, had been ruined.

The only light was filtering in from the neon and marquees and streetlamps outside, but Gordon could see plainly just how much damage had been done. He himself was the only unscathed item in the place. Thousands upon thousands of dollars, and many days of work, would have to be invested to put this bullet-torn Humpty Dumpty back together. And now the anger pushed away the tears. He wasn't thinking about the money. He was thinking about the greedy bastards who did this.

Glass crunching under his shoes, he walked to the phone, at the counter, but the phone was among much else that had been shot apart.

He found his way outside—the double glass front doors were a ruptured metal framework now—into a warm night, where a few people were gathering, but not many. He looked at his watch: after three A.M. He'd slept a long time before his machine-gun wake-up call. He was wondering where he could find a phone at this time of night, and if he could whether he should call the police or not, when the sirens cut the air almost as dramatically as the machine-gun fire had before it.

He felt calm now; strangely calm. He found a package of cigarettes in his breast pocket and some matches, too. He lit up a smoke.

The two uniformed policemen seemed young—two of those rookies Eliot Ness had brought onto the force, with much fanfare not so long ago, he supposed—and he told them everything that had happened. No, he hadn't gotten a look at the car or the driver; it was a dark sedan of some kind, that was all he made out in the short time before he ducked under the table. No, he didn't think it was a murder attempt—he didn't think whoever did it realized he, Gordon, was even on the premises.

"How do you read it, then, Mr. Gordon?" the slightly older of the two cops asked.

"Simple vandalism," he said, shrugging, smoking.

"Do you have any idea who might have done this?" the other cop asked.

"Any idea at all why you were singled out for this?" the first cop added.

And here was where his cooperation had to stop.

"No," Gordon said, and smiled meaninglessly. "None."

And he had asked to be excused. His wife would be worried about him, he said.

Actually, she wouldn't be. She was used to his long

and odd hours; and she was in fact deep asleep and didn't wake when he crawled into bed. He didn't tell her about the machine-gunning till the next morning, over breakfast, and even then didn't tell her that he'd been in the line of fire, or in any danger at all, for that matter. He told her less, in fact, than he'd told the two rookie cops.

This was business, after all. And the fear, tears, and anger of the night before needed to be kept to himself. Not forgotten, never forgotten; but tucked away. The most important order of business was business. Was getting his restaurant put back together.

Shortly after ten that morning, Vernon Gordon, in a well-tailored blue suit with a blue-and-white tie snug at his throat, looking nothing at all like a man who the night before had recoiled under a table while gunfire chewed up the world above him, entered the third-floor offices of the union headquarters in a turn-of-the-century, six-story brick building on East Seventeenth Street. He walked without a word past an attractive young brunette secretary who was doing the morning filing (of her nails) at a reception desk in the small, sparsely furnished waiting room, and entered a large, sparsely furnished office where Big Jim Caldwell sat with feet up on a desk as he read the sports section of the morning paper. He was smoking a cigar.

As if at military attention, Gordon stood across the desk from Caldwell, who barely glanced up from the paper. The fat little man in shirt-sleeves said, not unpleasantly, "Good morning, Mr. Gordon. Paper says you suffered some vandalism last evening. Dirty shame."

"How much?" Gordon asked coldly.

Half hidden behind the papers, Caldwell said, "As terrible as these lawless vandals are, I feel sure they didn't realize you were in the restaurant. I'm sure no one would have wanted you to come to harm."

"How much?"

Looking up from the paper, smiling slightly around his cigar, the round-faced Caldwell said, "The other day I gave you advice and you didn't listen. A shame."

"How much?"

He folded the paper and placed it gently across his generous lap. "You see, as it turned out, you could've used that bulletproof glass."

"How much?"

"You should take this opportunity to put some in. Bulletproof glass, I mean."

"How much?"

Caldwell, his expression blandly pleasant, shrugged. "Same as before."

"You already got fifteen hundred out of me. And the window washers union fee."

"That covers work—and plate glass—from days past. We're discussing the present, right now, and the future. You have a remodeling job to do, and you're going to need carpenters, glaziers, the whole megillah. You need the unions I control. You need me." He gestured to himself with a pudgy hand, two fingers of which now held the cigar. "And I need two thousand dollars."

"I should turn your fat ass over to the cops."

Caldwell's expression remained pleasant, but it was as hard and transparent as the plate glass he peddled. "I'm sure that would give you a certain satisfaction. The question is, would it replace the satisfaction of successfully opening your new restaurant? Because without me in your corner, you're out of fucking business, laddie-buck."

Gordon contained his rage; he stood, as if frozen, and said, "I'll have the money for you this afternoon. In cash."

Caldwell unfolded the paper, lifted it off his lap. "Good. Give me a call, and we'll arrange a drop. Little Jim'll pick it up. And I'll see to it that you get your bulletproof glass."

Gordon raised a cautionary finger. "I view this as a business expense. I'm putting up with it as such. Push me one step beyond this point and I'll consider you a bad investment. I *will* see your fat ass in jail, and it *will* give me considerably more than just a 'certain' satisfaction."

Caldwell smiled like a cherub. "You've made your point. We understand each other." He raised the paper, blocking his face from Gordon's view.

But Gordon figured the cherubic smile was gone when the voice from behind the paper said: "Don't come here again. Union headquarters is for union members only."

"What a pity I can't belong to such an elite club," Gordon said, and stalked out.

9

Ness stood in the midst of the wreckage of the Gordon's restaurant on Playhouse Square, hat pushed back, hands on his hips, face tightened into a mask of disgust. Sunlight streamed through the rows of yawning metal mouths where plate glass had been, sun glinting and bouncing off their jagged teeth.

"Chicago typewriter wrote this," Will Garner said, pointing to the patterns of bullet holes in the woodwork, the plaster. The big Indian in a brown suit was slowly prowling the shard-strewn, rubble-filled dining room.

Detective Albert Curry, tagging along after Ness, seemed shaken. He had apparently never seen the damage a machine gun could do.

"We've had broken windows before," Curry said, "but nothing like this. This goes beyond vandalism into sheer . . ."

He searched for a sufficient word.

"Gangsterism," Ness filled in flatly. "This is extortion in the true, time-honored Black Hand tradition. This is how the Mafia got its start, gentlemen."

"We aren't dealing with the Mafia, surely," Curry said with a nervous smile. "This is labor racketeering, pure and simple."

"It's labor racketeering, all right," Ness said, kneeling, picking up several blunted .45 slugs and dropping them into an evidence envelope. "But it's not pure and it's not simple."

Garner said, "I think Mr. Gordon's arrived."

Ness stood and watched as Vernon Gordon, wearing a

84

blue suit and a scowl, stepped inside his shot-out front doors and heaved a sigh.

"I thought I'd covered this last night," Gordon said impatiently, not meeting the eyes of Ness or Curry or Garner. "I gave a full statement to the two officers."

Ness walked over, glass fragments fragmenting further under his feet, and smiled tightly at Gordon and said, "Good morning, Vern."

The two men knew each other socially, at the country club, at various business and fraternal associations around town; they were less than friends, but hardly strangers.

"Sorry, Eliot," Gordon said with a quick smile, still not meeting Ness's gaze. "Afraid I'm a little testy this morning."

"I can well understand why."

He gestured with both hands, indicating his ravaged restaurant. "But, frankly, I have a lot to do—obviously. I've said all I have to regarding this ... accident."

"Accident? Why, did somebody accidentally fire off a few hundred rounds of forty-five caliber ammunition your way? That's a hell of an accident, Vern."

"Eliot, I have things to attend to."

"You sure as hell do. You need to attend to the bastards responsible. And I'm here to offer my help in that regard."

Gordon sighed, and he smiled again, wearily. "I'm grateful. But I'm afraid there's nothing either of us can do."

"Why don't you tell me about your union troubles, Vern."

"I don't have any union troubles, Eliot." He sighed again, adding, almost to himself, "Not now."

"I see. Then you've talked to Caldwell and/or McFate already this morning."

Gordon said nothing.

Ness gestured with a fist. "You can help me put those venal bastards away. This episode goes way beyond anything they've pulled to date. Firing off machine guns in the city streets is not going to endear the public—or a judge or a jury—to the 'boys.' This time they've gone too far."

Gordon was shaking his head side to side, as if Ness's

words were blows he needed to deflect. "Eliot, I didn't see who did it."

"You could have been killed, Vern."

"Whoever did it didn't realize I was here."

"That wouldn't make you any less dead."

"Well, I'm not dead."

Ness raised a hand as if swearing an oath in court. "It was late at night—or in the early morning hours, depending on how you look at it."

"Yes."

"So it was well after the theater crowd on Euclid had cleared. The streets were fairly empty."

"That's right."

"According to the officers' report, the car—a dark sedan—stopped, and then someone fired upon your restaurant. Is that right?"

"Well . . . yes."

"As opposed to firing while the car drove by?"

"I'd say that's right. Why? What's the significance of that?"

Garner, who had ambled over near Ness, said, "It means there was only one man in the car, most likely. He had to come to a stop, slide over and shoot."

Gordon looked confused. "Is that significant?"

"I think so," Ness said. "I don't think either Caldwell or McFate would do the machine-gunning themselves, so it required strong-arm assistance. To which end they only used one man."

Gordon's irritation was barely in check; but he couldn't disguise his interest, either. "So what?"

Curry, standing next to his chief, said, "Our understanding of the approach McFate and Caldwell take, when putting the squeeze on the likes of yourself, is to do everything themselves, from first contact to payoff. They like to keep the circle small."

"Using one man as their strong-arm," Garner explained, "fits that same pattern. They used one man on what most would consider at least a two-man job. Keeping the circle tight, and small."

"Vern," Ness said, "you've done a lot for Cleveland. Do something more—help us get rid of this sickness."

Gordon's eyes tightened and his reluctance to turn Ness down was apparent, but nonetheless he shook his head no.

"We can give you and your family police protection," Curry said. "We can watch the restaurant, too."

Ness nodded, confirming what Curry said, finally catching Gordon's eyes and locking on to them. "You can help rid Cleveland and its business community of one hell of an embarrassment."

The sunlight streaking through the room caught Gordon in the face and he winced; he moved till his face was out of the light and then he looked at Ness with eyes that were tired and sad and resigned to it all.

"Like everybody else in the business community," Gordon said, "I need to stay in business. I do what I have to do to do that."

Ness had an edge in his tone. "And you don't think putting Caldwell and McFate in jail would be good for business?"

"Eliot, I can't help you on this one. I have contractors to call; I have much to put in motion. I have a restaurant to open. If you'll excuse me."

Gordon, glass snapping under his shoes, exited through a bullet-scarred doorway that led to a stairway.

The three detectives stood in the rubble-scattered room, looked at each other and, with the precision of choreography, shrugged.

Ness picked up a chair, glanced at it to see if it was more or less intact, shook some crushed glass and detritus from its seat, and sat down. He nodded to Garner and Curry to find chairs and sit, and they did.

"We need Vern Gordon," Ness said. "I'll keep working on him. I'll talk to the mayor and see if he and Frank Darby, the Chamber of Commerce president, can't apply some pressure."

"I hope they have better luck than Will and I," Curry said glumly.

Ness looked at Garner, who shrugged with his eyebrows. "No luck?" he asked them.

Curry pulled his pocket notebook and began to thumb through it. "Over the past several days, we've talked to several dozen merchants who've been victims of vandalism that seems to be union-related."

"A number of them were willing to speak off the record," Garner said, "but no one wants to buck the unions and talk to a grand jury."

"That new shoe store on Euclid, they were hit up for a grand," Curry said. "It was the same tactic the boys no doubt pulled here at the restaurant: threatening to pull the union glaziers off the job, leaving 'em windowless on the eve of their big opening."

"Our friends hit the smaller businesses, too," said Garner.

Curry nodded, leafing through the notebook, stopping here and there to point out an example. "Here's a fashion shop, also on Euclid, that paid Caldwell a hundred-buck 'fine' because they had some nonunion painting done. And a soda shop paid a fifty-buck 'fine' because the owner allowed his cousin to paint a storeroom, and a butcher who paid 'em sixty bucks because he used nonunion labor to install some fixtures. And a clothing store that, during a work halt, coughed up five hundred for a fund for unemployed union workers."

"That," Garner said with a quiet sarcasm, "was in return for Caldwell and McFate settling a 'jurisdictional dispute' between two unions."

"What about this 'jurisdictional dispute' business?" Curry asked Ness. "Is there anything to it?"

"Phony as a three-dollar bill," Ness said, shaking his head no. "A real jurisdictional dispute is settled by arbitration, and work on jobs continues until the arbitration is settled."

"We haven't talked to everybody," Garner said. "We may get somebody willing to talk on the record, yet."

"If we could convince Vernon Gordon," Ness said, "the rest would fall in line."

Curry glanced around at the shot-up room. "This is the one to nail 'em on. We got a lot of photographs this morning; they'll look great blown up as court exhibits."

A voice from behind them said, "What did I miss?"

They turned to see Sam Wild, in a red bow tie and pale yellow seersucker suit and straw fedora, grinning at them through the framing of a shot-out window.

Ness motioned for Wild to join them, and he did, coming around through the front double doors that were barely there. He found a chair on the floor, set it upright, brushed it off and sat on it backward, leaning up against the back of it.

"Some air-conditioning system this joint has," he said wryly, noting the sunshine shooting in. "I bet our safety director's feeling homesick."

"Homesick?" Curry asked.

Ness said, "I think he means this place ought to remind me of Chicago."

Wild nodded, grinned wolfishly, dug a pack of Lucky Strikes out of a pocket. Lighting up a smoke, he said, "Looks like the Hawthorne Hotel's coffee shop the day Hymie Weiss tried to have Capone splattered."

"You're a sentimental soul, Sam," Ness said.

"Has Gordon been around? I'd like to interview him. We got some dandy photos this morning, but the great entrepreneur himself wasn't around."

"Gordon came in not long ago," Ness said. "He's upstairs in his office, I'd imagine. I don't think he'll want to talk to you."

"He's not cooperating with the Department of Public Safety?"

"He's not uncooperative."

"But he's not cooperative, either."

"You could say that."

"Yeah, but not in print." He shrugged. "The Gordon family are big advertisers. You know, these clowns Caldwell and McFate've got everybody scared—and now this machine-gun nonsense—brother. You're going to have a hell of a time getting anybody to testify."

"You're telling us," Curry said.

"I think we can give you a list of merchants," Ness said, "who might be willing to talk off the record."

"Yeah, that'd be something, anyway," Wild said reflectively, blowing out smoke. "We could do a nice big exposé on the 'boys.' That might build some nice public pressure."

"Worth a try," Ness said. "You can get the names from Detective Curry."

"Any other ideas? We dissipated denizens of the Fourth Estate need all the help we can get from our public officials."

"Go around and see Jack Whitehall," Ness said casually.

Both Garner and Curry looked sharply, with some surprise, at their boss.

"The Teamster?" Wild asked, equally surprised. "That thug?"

"He's no angel," Ness said, "but unlike Caldwell and McFate, his goals are rooted in something more than just making a buck. He really believes in the union ideals. He's no shakedown artist, and I've heard he resents the two Jims."

"Are you serious?" Wild asked, smiling, eyes narrowed, thinking Ness might be stringing him along.

"Give it a try," Ness said, with a little shrug.

Wild lifted his eyebrows and put them back down. "Oh-kay," he said.

The reporter and Curry sat and put their heads together for a few minutes as the young detective gave Wild a list of merchants, with words of guidance on each.

Then the lanky reporter rose, stretched, yawned, and pitched his spent cigarette to the glass-littered floor.

"See you in church, kids," he said, and ambled out.

"Do you trust him?" Garner asked. The Indian was watching Wild's departing back through the row of windowless windows, as if considering whether or not to put an arrow or maybe a tomahawk between the reporter's shoulder blades.

"Yes, Will, I trust him," Ness said. "So should you."

Garner shrugged, smiled a little. "Okay. I trust him."

Curry said, "What's the next step? Do we keep at the merchants?"

"Not just now. Let's let some of that public pressure Mr. Wild mentioned build up some. I have another assignment for the two of you."

They looked at him expectantly.

"We know that Caldwell and McFate handle almost every aspect of their shakedowns themselves. Certainly they make all the initial contacts themselves, and take the payoffs."

"A small circle," Garner said, nodding.

"Let's widen that circle some," Ness said, with a nasty smile. "Let's put a twenty-four-hour watch on Big Jim and Little Jim. I'll get several more shifts of two-man teams, assigned 'round the clock."

"And, what?" Curry asked. "Try to catch them in the act?"

"No. I want you to make no pretense of hiding your presence. Get on their fat butts and stay there. Our goal here is deterrence, not surveillance. From now on, Mr. Caldwell and Mr. McFate will be chaperoned by the city—they'll have their own private police escort."

"I like it," Garner said, the thinnest of smiles on his bronze face.

"But we can't catch them at something that they aren't doing anymore," Curry said, confused.

"We don't need them to commit any new crimes," Ness said. "They committed plenty already. We'll keep working on Vern Gordon and other potential witnesses, both here in Cleveland and outside the city as well. I'll be building a case, gentleman, while you keep on theirs."

The three men exchanged smiles and rose and exited the restaurant into a sunny morning just as a contractor, several carpenters, painters, and plasterers were unloading trucks out front.

10

Little Jim McFate, after a week of it, was not amused.

He wasn't known for his sense of humor, anyway; in fact, Big Jim often kidded him about being such a gloomy Gus. But Little Jim knew that the labor racket was a serious one; that when you were organizing, you had to paint a black picture of what life without unions was like. That when you were running a shakedown, for instance, you had to make the mark believe you really would break his legs. And then you really had to break them, if it come to that.

Nothing funny about it. He hadn't got to this exalted position by being some half-assed prankster. Like when he formed the protective association for the barbers of Cleveland, where he clipped the barbers for dues while elevating and fixing prices. You had to be tough, sharp, and taken seriously, to pull off that kind of scam.

So Little Jim's no-nonsense manner had come in handy, over the years. But he liked a good time as much as the next fellow. The workers he represented—painters, carpenters, glaziers, and the rest—thought he was swell. They knew he was a down-to-earth guy who would sell you the shirt off his back and gladly hoist a few with you.

And it wasn't like he didn't enjoy a good laugh—he liked "Jiggs and Maggie" in the funnies, and Laurel and Hardy at the movies, although the dirty stories you heard in bars made him uncomfortable. He was a family man, after all. A husband. A father.

He had fond memories of his own childhood, though memories of his father, who died when Jim was six, were few. Pop, a carpenter, had worked himself to death trying to support the McFate brood. Growing up on the West Side, in a working-class neighborhood, Little Jim learned early on that there were goddamn few opportunities to make it out, to make it big. He watched his older brothers work their tails off, getting cheated out of good wages by the factories where they toiled, and swore it would never happen to him.

Real wealth, he could see, came not from hard work, but from theft. Some thieves were thieves; some were mob guys; while others were robber barons, or bankers. And Little Jim had learned, also, early on, that there would never be an opening for him on a steel mill's board of directors, or at a bank.

When he got back from the war, he got a painting crew going, and noticed that not only his business, but all business, was booming. Consequently, unions seemed like a place where some good could be done, and some money could be made. He signed a lot of painters up for the local, and put together a really nice con on the side, selling permits to home owners who wanted to paint their own homes. If a home owner didn't buy a permit, Little Jim would wait till the house was painted and then splash stain all over it.

That con, after years of moneymaking, finally got shut down last year, when Little Jim's front man got nailed by the safety director's dicks. But it was sweet while it lasted.

So, anyway, it wasn't like Little Jim McFate had no sense of humor.

And when this goddamn thing had first begun, he'd even allowed Big Jim to convince him it was a big joke.

"They're following us around, everywheres we go," Little Jim had said after a full day of it, two days after the Gordon's restaurant shooting. He was pacing around Big

Jim's office at union headquarters on East Seventeenth Street.

Caldwell had his feet on the desk and his hands behind his head, elbows flaring out, a big grin on his face and a big cigar in his grin.

"Laddie-buck," Caldwell said, eyes twinkling like a goddamn pixie's, "the great Mr. Eliot Ness has gone and done us an honor."

"An *honor?*" Little Jim halted his pacing.

"He's put us under police protection. To make sure no harm comes our way."

"Judas priest, man. How can you take this so lightly?"

Big Jim swung his feet off the desk; he flicked ashes off his cigar into an ashtray that was one of the few objects on the desk. There were no papers or anything else to indicate work was ever done on that smooth oak surface.

"I don't take it lightly," he said, standing, strolling over to McFate. "But we're the subject of some very bad press right now. We can use this police attention to our betterment."

"To our betterment? What in the hell—"

"Boyo—look. We took extreme measures with Mr. Vernon Gordon. They were necessary, and I think they'll in future make our efforts with other downtown merchants go even quicker, even smoother. But right now the newspapers are engaging in some nasty speculation. About us."

"They're all but goddamn coming out and saying we did it!"

"Well, we did."

"Like hell! I was home in bed, asleep with my missus!"

"Bucko, we had it done. And that is a fact."

Big Jim shrugged. "Well, sure. We had it done. Of course we had it done. We should sue the bastards for slander!"

Caldwell put a hand on his partner's shoulder, patted it in a there-there fashion. "It's libel, only it isn't libel when it's true, and so we're not going to make a bad situation worse by acknowledging those accusations."

"It's that bastard Wild. He's in Ness's pocket."

"So he is. But the other papers have picked up on it as well. We're the top-billed act of the editorial pages these days."

"And now we got goddamn cops trailing us all over town! Trailing me home! It's embarrassing! I'm a goddamn family man."

"I know you are, lad. As am I. But there's no harm done by this attention."

"No harm! How are we expected to do business when—"

Caldwell frowned, shook his head no, vigorously. "We aren't going to do any business. Not any new business. Now's not a good time for that, anyway, not with a press spotlight on us. And we'll have our regular payoffs picked up by people we trust. Harry Gibson needs something to do with his hands."

"I thought you gave him a job at your glass warehouse."

"I did. But he can use that as a place to work out of."

Now Little Jim was the one shaking his head no. "I don't like getting too many people involved. I like to keep the business end to just the two of us."

Caldwell shrugged with one shoulder. "Gibson's already involved."

"Well, he's an all right ghee," Little Jim admitted. "But let's not pass out too many invites to the party."

"Agreed," Caldwell said, nodding.

"Far as I'm concerned," Little Jim went on, "we got two uninvited guests already, all the time."

He was referring to the two cops who were constantly on their tails.

"Actually," said Caldwell, "I think there's six of 'em—three shifts of two. Think of the money we're costing the taxpayers. After a week or so of lawful activities, we might point out to some reporter—and I don't mean Sam Wild—that Mr. Ness is wasting precious tax dollars."

Now Little Jim began to smile, a little. "You mean,

we use the cops hanging onto us to show that we're not doing anything wrong."

Big Jim nodded. "That's exactly right—not doing anything but going about union business, upright moral representatives of the working man."

"Will the papers run that?"

"Sure they will. They need a new story every day. That story about us being bad boys will be old before you know it. Eliot Ness is a big shot in the papers, but remember—the next day they wrap fish in 'im."

That made Little Jim laugh. That was a good one.

"Besides," Caldwell said, grabbing his derby, "we can have a little fun with our chaperons."

"Fun?"

"Just follow me," Caldwell said, grinning, pausing only to relight his cigar before swaggering out of the union offices and heading for the street.

And for the better part of a week Big Jim, and Little Jim, too, indeed had fun with their police retinue.

The boys made a habit of taking long drives in the country, in a new Buick owned by the union (but used by Big Jim—a matching Buick owned by the union was Little Jim's to use). The cops were driving old clunkers and had trouble keeping up with the sleek, powerful sedans. Big Jim would step on the gas and take the car to the edge of the speed limit, over rough, bumpy backroads, making the cops work to keep up, their buggies shimmying and shaking and rattling. Sometimes the two Jims would lose their escorts and have to pull over to the side of the road and wait, or slow to a gawking Sunday driver's pace, till Cleveland's finest caught up.

Similar hijinks marked their in-town pleasure driving. Big Jim would take it easy, then round a corner and slip into an alley before the cops had made the turn; then Big Jim would wait for them to go by, pull in behind the shadows and honk, startling and embarrassing them.

It was good for a laugh, for a while. But Little Jim got sick of it quickly, and, finally, after almost a week of it, so did Big Jim.

And now, at the beginning of another day that held as its only prospect driving aimlessly around the Cleveland area with cop magnets stuck to their asses, Big Jim was the one pacing around the union office, while Little Jim sat glumly behind the desk, frustration and boredom eating at him.

"I thought they'd give it up by now," Caldwell said. He was smoking a cigar again, but puffing nervously at it, like the smokestack of a train engine taking a steep grade.

"And the papers haven't taken the bait," Little Jim said.

Big Jim shook his head side to side in bewilderment. "I thought they would. I really thought they would. Us leading those jerks on wild goose chases out in the sticks, that's good stuff. They oughta use it, goddamn it."

Dour Little Jim leaned his long face on one hand, elbow propped against the uncluttered desktop. "Why should they? You plant the story in a few reporters' ears, but how do they know it's for real? They got to see it with their own eyes."

And now Big Jim stopped in his tracks and grinned. He pointed with the stubby cigar at his partner, like he was aiming a projectile. "You, my friend, are more than just a pretty face."

"Huh?"

"You gave me an idea. You gave me one hell of an idea."

The chunky Caldwell fired himself at the desk like a cannonball. His charge was so quick it took McFate aback.

"You're gonna love this," Caldwell said, grinning like a demented cherub. "You're gonna just love it."

Little Jim would reserve judgment on that, but he watched, spellbound, as his associate whirled into action, making one phone call after another.

Shortly before noon, just hours and a flurry of activity later, Big Jim Caldwell and Little Jim McFate walked out into the glorious, sunny August day. One would think they had stepped not out of a six-story brick building, but a bandbox. They were dressed in black silk top hats that reflected the sunlight, striped trousers and swallow-tailed coats, vests with white piping, and Ascot ties snugged under wing collars. Their black shoes, peeking out from under pearl-gray spats, outshone the sun. Both carried gold-crowned walking sticks like scepters. They looked as grand as two petty crooks decked out in rental attire could ever hope to look.

Grander.

Parked at the curb were two glistening black Packard touring cars, their tops down; a colored chauffeur in uniform stood at attention, holding open the rear door of the first of the two Packards. Big Jim gestured regally for Little Jim to enter first. Little Jim did, and Big Jim followed, and the chauffeur shut the door with a satisfying metallic *chunk* and took his position behind the wheel.

The second Packard, directly behind the first, was filled with a small but formally dressed musical group: a trumpet, a trombone, a clarinet, and a snare drum. The colored chauffeur of the second car had a glazed, wide-eyed look, like a black comedian in the movies. But his eyes were no wider, his expression no more glazed, than that of the two plainclothes police officers in the car parked in front of union headquarters, taking all of this in.

Little Jim recognized the cop in the rider's seat as Albert Curry, one of the safety director's dicks. Neither he nor Big Jim knew the name of the other one, a big dark fellow who looked like an Indian, but they had come to know his face well. He and Curry had been their day-shift companions since the first day of the surveillance.

"Driver," Caldwell said, "let the parade begin."

And the first Packard pulled away from the curb, the second one slowly falling in line, with the two cops trailing after in their clunker of a black Ford sedan.

"You know," Caldwell said, smiling almost sweetly, leaning his head so close to his partner their top hats touched, "Ness embarrassed Snorkey once. Snorkey went apeshit and starting busting stuff up."

"Snorkey?"

"Ah. You don't go back that far with the Outfit, do

you, lad? Snorkey. Capone. Ness wanted to get some press attention, he wanted to embarrass Big Al. So he took all of the beer trucks that he and his so-called 'untouchables' confiscated and they had a big parade up Michigan Avenue, right past the Lexington Hotel, where they knew Snorkey would be watching. Fifty or sixty of the goddamn things. Just to give Snorkey the needle—and get in the papers."

"Got a lot of attention, I'll bet."

"Parades always do, bucko. Parades always do."

And the three-car convoy made its way down Euclid Avenue, at noon, a slow procession that was taken in by laughing lunch-hour spectators, and the photographers of the press who had been tipped by Big Jim, who along with Little Jim tipped his silk hat regally to the amazed, amused crowds, who began to stop and line up along the sidewalks, waving back, some of them even cheering.

Hoots of laughter filled the air as the curb-lined gallery read the banner draped across the rear of the first touring car:

CALDWELL AND MCFATE'S CIRCUS
COURTESY THE DEPARTMENT OF PUBLIC SAFETY
CITY OF CLEVELAND

At East Fourth Street the motorcade paused at the scene of a fender-bender accident: two taxis had crashed into each other, and the drivers were out, talking to a pair of uniformed cops. A small crowd had gathered, who now looked gleefully toward the Caldwell and McFate fleet. Little Jim, as they passed by the accident scene, noted that the windshield of one vehicle was spiderwebbed.

Impulsively he shouted: "Hey—there ain't supposed to be no window smashing today, boys!"

Howls and guffaws burst from the outdoor audience, and Big Jim patted the taller man on the back, knocking Little Jim's top hat off balance.

"To think I ever accused you of havin' no sense of humor," Caldwell said.

Little Jim smiled like the Mona Lisa and damn near blushed.

And, of course, while all of this was unfolding, Curry and the Indian were bringing up the rear, the younger cop's face crimson with embarrassment. The car they were immediately tailing was the one bearing the musicians, a mere combo to be sure, but, small as they were, putting out a lot of sound.

Specifically, they were playing "Me and My Shadow."

11

While Caldwell and McFate's "Big Parade" (as the press would soon call it) was still under way, Eliot Ness was finishing a quiet lunch at the Cleveland Hotel's posh Bronze Room, where in a back booth he and his executive assistant, Bob Chamberlin, were going over a travel itinerary.

"As far as anybody else is concerned," Ness said, keeping his voice down, his eyes locking Chamberlin's, "this trip is strictly to confer with the Buffalo officials on matters of traffic control."

Chamberlin sipped his coffee, nodded. "Particularly the news hounds."

"Yes—including Sam Wild. Including the rest of our staff, for that matter. Have you made the appointments?"

Chamberlin nodded again. "You'll start off with a contractor named Phillips."

"He was cooperative on the phone?"

"Very. I think he'll testify, once he's met with you and sized you up. He says he tried to do business in Cleveland over the past several years, but finally gave it up because of the 'extras' that were cropping up."

"'Extras.'" Ness shook his head in disgust. "Specifically, bribes, payoffs, and phony 'fines' that went to line Caldwell's and McFate's pockets."

"Precisely." Chamberlin's ironic smile was smaller than his tiny mustache. "Phillips has a major construction business in Buffalo—he's engaged in building a chain of gas stations in a dozen cities right now, for the Tydol people—and he said to me, and I quote, 'You couldn't get me to Cleveland if I got a

101

five-million-dollar contract, because the racketeers would have it all before I got through.'"

Ness raised an eyebrow. "Well, let's hope we can get him to Cleveland to talk to a grand jury."

"I think you can sell him on it. He's got a lot of bitterness toward the 'boys.' Now, next on the Buffalo agenda are two smaller contractors, home builders who—"

Ness, sitting with his back to the wall, as was his habit, raised a hand in a stop motion. "Hold up, Bob. Here comes Albert Curry."

"Curry?" Chamberlin said disbelievingly, craning his neck around to see for himself. "Isn't he on the detail that's keeping tabs on Big Jim and Little Jim?"

"He's supposed to be," Ness said, a hint of irritation in his voice, but curiosity, too.

Curry approached the booth and, hat in hands, looking sheepish but clearly angry, planted his feet and stood as if at parade rest. "I'm sorry to interrupt your lunch."

"We've had our lunch, Albert," Ness said. "Why don't you sit down and not attract any more attention than you already have and tell us what you're doing here."

Curry swallowed and slid into the booth next to Chamberlin. "I figured this is where you'd be. I had Garner let me out, and walked over. He's still on the job."

"Then our subjects are still under surveillance?"

"Oh yes. Look, Chief, I'm sorry to walk off the job and barge in on your—"

"Albert. Spill."

Albert spilled. In a rush he told of the humiliating procession he'd so recently been a part of.

Chamberlin laughed humorlessly. "Those bastards certainly have their nerve."

Ness smiled faintly. "They just have a sense of humor. Well, you know something? So have I."

Curry began to smile, now, liking the sound of that.

"You know," Ness said, pushing aside a half-eaten piece of pecan pie, "it seems to me that we've put the Kingsbury Run investigation on the back burner long enough."

Both Curry and Chamberlin looked at Ness in frank confusion.

"What in God's name," Chamberlin said, "has the Mad Butcher of Kingsbury Run got to do with—"

"Bob," Ness said pleasantly, pragmatically, "I want you to call Sergeant Merlo and have him pull some boys off the detective bureau. You know, the Butcher has been preying upon vagrants and the so-called dregs of humanity. It occurs to me that today would be a fine day to round up fifty or so of the filthiest vagrants in town, to question in our ongoing investigation."

Chamberlin began to smile slowly.

"Now since the Butcher only strikes at the most unfortunate of society's outcasts, naturally we needn't question anyone who appears to have had a bath within, oh, say... the previous three months."

"Naturally," Chamberlin said, toasting Ness with a coffee cup, then sipping from it.

"Have Merlo do this at once," Ness said. "And have him put them all in the same holding tank in the central jail."

"I got you," Chamberlin said, setting the cup down, nodding to Curry, who slid back out of the booth to allow Chamberlin to be on his way.

"Bob?"

Chamberlin turned. "Yes?"

"How long will this process take, would you think?"

"Not very. Three hours at the outside."

"Fine. Go to it."

Curry was still not following this. His own smile had long since faded.

"Chief," he said, "I have nothing against reactivating the Butcher investigation... God knows I never thought that guy Dolezal was guilty anyway, but why *now*?"

Ness leaned across the booth. "Albert," Ness said to the young detective, "wouldn't you say you witnessed a flagrant example of the law being broken today?"

"Huh?"

"Disturbing the peace. Don't you think that two representatives of rank-and-file union members would know better than to disrupt the lunch hour of Cleveland's citizens with some noisy, traffic-clogging 'parade'?"

And Curry finally got it. "Yes, yes . . . definitely a law was broken. And they didn't have a permit for a public display like that."

"Well, you should make sure first. Check at the county clerk's office at City Hall. It should take you, oh . . . about three hours."

Curry was nodding, grinning.

And Ness's smile turned very nasty. "Then I want you to go up to that union office and arrest Big Jim and Little Jim, or if they're still parading around in a touring car, pull them over . . . but either way, throw their fat asses in jail. In a certain holding tank."

Curry was grinning like a Cheshire cat, now. Without a word, he scurried out of the Bronze Room. Ness, pleased with himself, ordered a Scotch.

Around four-thirty that afternoon, back in his office, Ness was at work cleaning up administrative paperwork to clear the way for his upcoming two-day Buffalo excursion. There was a characteristic (shave-and-a-haircut-two-bits) knock, which he recognized as Sam Wild's at the private-entry hall door. He rose from his rolltop desk and unlocked the door and Wild stumbled in, like a drunk.

Only he was intoxicated with laughter, not booze. Tears were streaming down his face.

"Hello, Sam," Ness said.

Wild, unable to speak, waved at Ness, found a chair over by one of the conference tables, and draped himself in it, long legs sticking out like a scarecrow's. The reporter laughed and laughed, finally digging a handkerchief out of a pocket to wipe his eyes and blow his nose.

"You are my hero," Wild said.

Ness was sitting back at the rolltop desk, with his chair swiveled around to face his friend. "Why, thanks. I do try to set an example for you. Give you something to shoot for."

"Well, I'll never top this." Wild's laughter had subsided, but he was grinning like a guy holding a winning sweepstakes ticket. "Busting Capone was nothin' compared to this."

"Compared to what, Sam?" Ness asked innocently.

Wild gestured over his shoulder with a thumb. "I was just over at the jail. Now I'll tell you what you already know, 'cause your fine hand is obvious in this: those smelly fuckin' bums you rousted on the Kingsbury Run case, there must be fifty or sixty of 'em, are sharing a cell with Big Jim and Little Jim, still decked out in their finery for that parade they put on today."

"No kidding."

"I never smelled anything so bad as those bums packed together in that holding tank. Pee-you! What a foul stench. And then somebody turned on the steam in the cell block, full blast. Every radiator in the joint was going."

Ness shrugged. "It is cool, for August."

"I mean, those guys smelled bad enough, before they got sweated out. And all the while Caldwell and McFate are going fuckin' nuts. They're screaming their lungs out. They look like a couple of corsages that got left out in the rain."

"I'm sure their lawyers will get them out soon enough."

"I'm sure. But oh you gave me a good laugh—and a great punch line for my story on the 'big parade.' They thought they were making suckers out of you, but they forgot the golden rule."

"Golden rule?"

"P.T. Barnum's. There's one born every minute. They made a sap out of you, but you made bigger saps out of them. My hat's off to you."

Ness leaned back in the chair. "I can't take credit for having the steam turned on."

"I'm sure that was that kid Al Curry's idea. He was hanging around, watching 'em like they was monkeys in the zoo. And they're grabbing onto the front bars like they are monkeys, too, in their wilted monkey suits."

Ness smiled and sighed. "I do wish I could see it."

Wild hauled himself up out of the chair, stretched, yawned. "Well, hell, they're probably sprung by now. Anyway, I got a story to write—thanks to you."

"Don't mention it. Have you, uh, talked to that Teamster yet?"

"Whitehall? Yeah. We made contact. You want details?"

"No."

Wild smirked. "Didn't think so. Why do I have the idea that you put the two of us together 'cause you think we share a common bond?"

"And what bond would that be?"

"Whitehall and me, we ain't either of us adverse to breaking a rule or two."

"Sam, I was just giving you a lead on what might make a good sidebar piece. Human interest."

"Right. I don't know what I was thinking of. Nothing you do *ever's* got an ulterior motive, does it?"

Wild tipped his straw fedora to the safety director, and slipped out into the hall; the press room was just down and across the way.

Ness went back to his desk and looked over the traffic statistics he'd need to be familiar with on the official leg of his Buffalo trip. He was just setting the material aside when he heard a commotion in his outer office. He rose and went to the door and peeked out on a room as large as his own; it was here that his secretary and several clerks kept desks and tended files, and responded to citizens who walked up to the wide counter with a complaint or request.

The two citizens who had bellied up to this bar had a complaint.

They were Big Jim Caldwell and Little Jim McFate, and they were still in their tuxes, although their top hats were long since abandoned and they looked like figures from a wedding cake—a stale one. Their finery looked wrinkled, withered, unwashed; their hair clung tight and yet haphazardly to their scalps, where it had dried after the drenching of sweat from the steamy jail cell.

And they smelled very bad indeed. They carried a cloud of body odor with them like a loser carried bad luck.

"We demand to see the safety director!" Caldwell was shouting. His voice was hoarse, his face devoid of blood.

Next to him, horse-faced, morose McFate was trembling with rage, like a child on the verge of tears.

The women in the outer office were taken aback by this loud, unsightly, malodorous intrusion—even Ness's efficient, redheaded secretary Wanda, who usually could ward off the most insistent and obnoxious constituent without batting an eye.

"You can't see Mr. Ness without an appointment," she was saying.

Ness stepped out into the outer office just far enough to be seen, smiled benignly and said, "Send the gentlemen in, Miss Goodson. They're old friends of mine."

He went into his office and stood with his arms folded, waiting. When the gamy, bedraggled pair entered—Caldwell first, McFate shutting the door rattlingly behind them—Ness gestured to two chairs at a nearby conference table.

Caldwell gestured no, with a violent motion. He said, "You think you're pretty goddamn cute."

"Frankly," Ness said pleasantly, "my being cute never occurred to me. My mother's accused me of that, from time to time, but just about nobody else ever has."

Caldwell pointed a finger like a gun; he said, through clenched teeth, "We can take anything you can dish out, pally, and throw it right back at you!"

"Oh," Ness said, sitting on the edge of the conference table, "I didn't realize that's why you dropped by."

"What?" Caldwell said.

"To confess. I can get my secretary in here and you can make a formal statement. You can begin with the Gordon's extortion and vandalism and work backward. . . ."

Caldwell sneered. "You don't need your girl, because we're not here to confess to shit. We came to say that you, Mayor Burton, and the Chamber of Commerce, and all the fat-cat industrialists in the city, are trying to ruin the labor movement. Well, it won't work, pally."

"Mr. Caldwell. Mr. McFate. If you have anything to do with the labor movement, that fact hasn't come to my attention as yet. And I've been examining your activities rather closely, gentlemen."

"Bring on your investigations," Caldwell said derisively, "bring on your indictments. You're bluffing. You haven't got a thing on us."

Ness said nothing; he just smiled blandly at the two disheveled men.

"Go ahead," McFate said, stepping forward ominously. "Do your worst, big shot."

"You boys have courage coming up here," Ness said. "I'll give you that."

"It's not courage," Caldwell said. "It's conviction. You're just part of the national attack on all labor by the moneyed interests, trying to weaken the movement by attacking aggressive leadership like us."

"Why don't you save the bullshit for the rank and file," Ness said coldly. "Although I doubt very many of them are buying it these days. Maybe you can find a paper to peddle it to."

Caldwell moved dangerously close to Ness. The stocky man's eyes were hard behind the wire-framed glasses. He said, "If you attack us like this again, pally, we'll stop you. Whatever it takes."

McFate said, "We'll stop you, you little prick."

"Boys," Ness said, going to his side door, opening it, and gesturing gently with one hand for them to make use of the exit, "haven't you heard about people in glass houses?"

They had no answer to that.

Gathering what remained of their dignity, but leaving a good deal of the smell behind, Big Jim and Little Jim stormed out. Ness shut the door hard on them—but not so hard as to break the pebbled glass. He'd hate like hell to have to replace it right now.

12

Sam Wild was nervous.

He wasn't a nervous man by disposition. In fact, he took most everything in stride; when you'd worked as many beats as he had, from politics to police, from four-alarm fires to auto fatalities, not much of anything shook you.

Tonight, he was shaking. Gently, but shaking, the match with which he was lighting his Lucky Strike trembling as if in a breeze, only there wasn't a breeze. It was a night (just after ten P.M.) as hot and dry as the back room of a bakery. The reporter was parked on East Seventeenth in a Chevy sedan that belonged to his paper, waiting for Jack Whitehall, the hard-nosed Teamster organizer who, it turned out, was a friend of Ness.

Of all things, of all people. Wild wondered if the day would ever come when Mr. Eliot Ness would run out of surprises for him. This time it was a real corker: the black sheep of the Cleveland labor scene turns out to be an old co-worker of the safety director's from a South Side Chicago factory. This one just about topped 'em all.

Over the past few days he and Whitehall had met several times in a saloon near the food terminal, where Whitehall had a major organizing effort under way. Whitehall had told Wild about the blacklist.

"So who's on this list, anyway?" Wild had asked.

"Stores that haven't cooperated with Caldwell and McFate," Whitehall said. "Businesses that aren't paying tribute to Caldwell's window washers union."

"So we're talking about windows that are going to get smashed."

"And windows that have already *been* smashed. Nobody on the blacklist can buy glass in the city of Cleveland— not till they come to terms with Big Jim and Little Jim."

"And Ness says a copy of this list would make his case."

"That's right. Only he doesn't know any legal way to get his hands on a copy."

Which, of course, was where Wild and Whitehall came in.

Wild smiled and sucked his Lucky, his third since he'd parked here. Without even coming out and asking, the safety director had relegated his dirty work to a member of the Fourth Estate and a representative of the local labor movement. Didn't that just about take the fucking cake.

And now here Wild sat, just down the block from the narrow six-story brick building where, on the third floor, Big Jim and Little Jim kept their union headquarters. At first he'd argued against ransacking Caldwell's office for the list.

"It'd be easier to pull one of 'em out of a glass-company office," Wild had said. "Those places are warehouse affairs, in industrial areas with easy access. You could probably walk right in during business hours, find a place to hide, and wait till—"

"No," Whitehall had said flatly. "The list would turn up missing and there'd be a stink. At the union there's gonna be multiple copies. There's got to be, 'cause Caldwell's giving the list to all the glass companies in town, and to whatever goon or goons are doing his window smashing for him. And then he's got to update it, periodically."

"So," Wild said, reluctantly seeing the logic of it, "you figure there's a stack of 'em someplace in Caldwell's office. We could grab one off the stack, and nobody'd be the wiser. It'd never be missed."

"Right."

Their objective, then, was the union headquarters in that nondescript six-story office building, one of many on the fringes of the downtown, the kind of marginal facility that thrived on mail-order companies, low-rent shysters, and abortionists. There would be no night watchman, and should be little trouble breaking in. Your classic lead-pipe cinch.

Only there was one major hitch: the building, on East Seventeenth near Payne, was about a block and a half from the Central Police Station. Cop cars were constantly cutting down Seventeenth from Payne to get to Euclid. An all-night, white-tile, one-arm restaurant in the next building, just across the alley, was frequented by a heavy police clientele. You couldn't find more cops this side of a Saint Paddy Day's parade.

So. In doing the unspoken bidding of the safety director—who, if his two friends were caught in the act, would no doubt profess disappointment in their lack of moral turpitude—Wild was preparing to burglarize a building within spitting distance of half the boys in blue in the city of Cleveland. What a dandy idea.

"Ready?"

Wild damn near dropped his Lucky in his lap, like to burn his nuts off. He hadn't seen or heard Whitehall approach. Now he looked over and the lantern-jawed, sleepy-eyed roughneck was framed in the car's open window on the rider's side. The bastard even seemed faintly amused.

"Sure," Wild said, with a nasty little smirk. "I'm always ready to risk my ass, and my paper's reputation, for the sake of unionism and Eliot fuckin' Ness."

"Come on, then."

Wild slipped out of the car and joined Whitehall on the sidewalk. Whitehall was wearing dark trousers and a dark blue work shirt with the sleeves rolled up on bulging biceps. Wild was wearing dark clothing himself, which was a change for him. But you don't wear white seersucker on burglaries.

The two men, both tall, Wild as lean as Whitehall was brawny, did not exactly make an inconspicuous pair as they walked down the deserted sidewalk along the busy street past the thriving, cop-filled one-arm joint. Several cops exited the restaurant, heading back to the Central Station on foot just as Wild and Whitehall were strolling by, but paid them no notice.

When the cops had rounded the corner, Whitehall and Wild ducked into the alley. From behind a garbage can, Whitehall withdrew a tool belt, which he slung around his waist; he tucked a pair of padded work gloves behind the tool belt. Then, standing fairly near the side of the building where the union headquarters was housed, Whitehall crouched, his feet planted firmly under him, and locked his hands together, palms up, and said, "Here."

"Where?"

Whitehall glowered and looked up sharply.

Above was the fire escape, which ran across the entire side wall of the building, forming black metal mesh Z's, ending a flight above the alley.

"Oh," Wild said, and put a foot in Whitehall's hands and allowed himself to be boosted to where he could pull down the counterbalanced fire escape stairs. As they swung down under Wild's grasp, Whitehall dodged out of the way, but reached out as he did to brace the stairs, so they didn't clang to the alley floor.

The two men paused, glancing out toward the sidewalk and street beyond the mouth of the alley, watching for cops.

Seeing none, Whitehall shrugged at Wild and Wild shrugged at Whitehall and they went on up the fire escape, the Teamster first. The stairs swung up after them as they went on up to the third floor level, where they walked along the catwalk to the window that looked in on Caldwell's office.

Nothing of the office could be seen, however, as the lights were off within and the window was burglar-proof wire glass.

Wild, already damp with sweat, whispered, "Got something on that tool belt to pry it open?"

"That sash is cast iron," Whitehall said. "I'm not sure I *could* pry it open, and if I did, it'd make a hell of a racket."

"What, then?"

Whitehall took a roll of masking tape from a pouch on the belt. He tore off long strips of the tape and began to cover the window with them. It seemed to Wild to take forever. The reporter could see the mouth of the alley from up here, and he kept glancing back that way. No cops.

When the window was crisscrossed with tape, till it seemed made more of tape than glass, Whitehall pulled his work gloves off the belt.

"How's it look?" Whitehall asked, snugging on the gloves.

Wild kept his eyes fixed on the mouth of the alley. "Fine."

Whitehall drew his fist back, about five inches from the center of the taped-over window; his bicep was tight and round and heavily veined.

Wild gripped Whitehall's shoulder.

Whitehall froze, glanced back. Two cops were standing at the mouth of the alley, talking. Their voices were barely audible, but then one of them laughed. The laughter echoed down the alley. Wild had plastered himself to the side of the building. Whitehall hadn't shifted his position, other than to relax his arm; but he was as motionless as a statue.

Footsteps resonated hollowly.

Wild held his breath, getting religion as the cop walked down the alley.

Whitehall remained inanimate as stone.

The cop stopped near the garbage cans below, where Whitehall had stowed his tool belt.

Wild couldn't see the man, now. The officer was under the fire escape, facing the building, that much Wild knew. He held his breath. Listened. Silence.

Then came the sound of a man pissing against a brick wall.

Tentatively, Wild allowed himself to breathe. The statue on the fire escape next to him began to smile, faintly.

Footsteps clip-clopped back up and out the alley, and the two cops were gone.

"That was some feat that bull pulled off," Whitehall said softly.

"Huh?"

"He emptied the piss out himself," Whitehall said, "and scared the piss out of me."

Wild smiled at that, and relaxed a little, then Whitehall smashed his fist into the taped-up window and Wild damn near fell off the 'scape.

But there wasn't much noise. A simple cracking was all.

They paused and waited, watching the alley again, seeing if anybody reacted to the sound, slight as it was.

No one did.

Whitehall returned to his work, picking out the pieces of glass, handing them to Wild, whose hands were cupped; but the wire mesh remained, and glass on the other side of the mesh clung.

"Fuck," Whitehall said. "I thought maybe I could make a hole and get my hand through and unlock this fucking thing. No such luck."

By this point Wild had a precarious house of shards in his cupped, gloveless hands.

"Go down and put those in one of the garbage cans," Whitehall said. "Quietly. Don't take your foot off the step, or the counterweight'll swing the 'scape up."

Wild swallowed and nodded and moved as quietly as he could along the wrought-iron walkway, maneuvering the stairs and keeping his balance though his bare hands were filled with jagged chips and chunks of glass. The most awkward part was getting the counterbalanced final flight of stairs to go down without spilling his brittle cargo, which he deposited as soundlessly as he could in the nearest open can, keeping one foot on the lower step. Then he went back up and got a second load of glass and repeated the procedure.

Whitehall was using wire cutters, clipping along the edges of the window at the wire mesh. Each little snip seemed loud as rifle shots to Wild, whose nervousness was turning into nausea. But the mouth of the alley remained empty of police, or anyone else, for that matter.

Finally Whitehall had snipped an upper corner area of the window sufficiently to push in the netting and the glass that clung to it; splinters and slivers of the already cracked glass gently showered the floor beyond. Whitehall rolled down his right sleeve, tucked the cuff under the glove and reached his hand in and around and unlatched the window.

Then they were over the sill and into Caldwell's office, the glass crackling under their heels. Whitehall left the window open behind them, but pulled the shade. Wild waited as his fellow trespasser walked across the dark room with the sureness of a blind man in his own home, and found the overhead light switch.

"Christ," Wild said, "wouldn't flashlights be better?"

"Why, did you bring some?"

"Well, no . . ."

"It would take forever with flashlights, Wild. With the lights on, we can make quick work of this."

"Where shall we start?"

"You take the desk. I'll take the file cabinets. Don't be tidy. We want 'em to think we were looking for money or valuables."

Wild nodded and went to work.

The desk was mostly empty. A box of Havana cigars, which Wild helped himself to a couple of, was about it. No sign of anything having to do with actual office work, let alone a box of blacklists.

Whitehall, standing at the oak file cabinets, was taking longer.

Wild called over to him, sotto voce. "Anything?"

"No. Just membership records, dues, some business ledgers. Standard stuff. Try that closet, why don't you?"

Wild went over and opened the closet door and said, "Shit."

"What is it?"

"A safe. A short fat squat safe."

Whitehall walked over and had a look. He said nothing.

"Safecracking isn't in my repertoire," Wild said. "How about you? Got some nitro in that tool belt?"

Whitehall looked the rest of the closet over; there were some shelves, but they were empty.

"Let's take a look out in the outer office," Whitehall said.

They went into the reception area, leaving the inner office door open, letting some light in, not turning on a light in there. Might attract a janitor's attention, Whitehall said.

"I'll take the desk," Whitehall said. "Check out that closet."

"If there's another safe in it, I'll spare you the sad news."

"Quiet," Whitehall said harshly, reaching over and pulling the door to the inner office mostly closed, putting the reception area into darkness.

Listening, Wild squinted in the dark, as if it would make him hear better.

Footsteps.

Then the familiar squeaking sound of a bucket and mop being pushed along. The flop and splash of the wet mop followed. The two men breathed easier, but they breathed quietly. If the cleaning woman out there heard them, noticed them in any way, that greasy spoon full of cops was only a scream away.

Wild was leaning on the knob of the closet door and Whitehall was sitting on the edge of the desk when the squeaking rolled on and faded and, finally, left them alone again.

Whitehall let some more light in from the inner office and said, "Nothing in the receptionist's drawers." Then he smiled. "Actually, I've seen the dame. There's plenty in her drawers."

Wild laughed a little at that; he was pleased to see some humor and humanity in the hulking Teamster. "Let me just finish up this closet," the reporter said.

It was a supply closet. Actual work was done out

here. Typing paper, ribbons, various forms and application blanks neatly boxed and shelved.

And, in a box on the upper shelf, a stack of stapled sheets; each document, four mimeograph pages in length, listed various merchants in the city of Cleveland. A cover sheet, on Window Washers Union letterhead, said, "The following have been deemed unfair to our local."

Wild took one copy and put the box back on its high shelf.

His nervousness was gone, but he was, suddenly, famished.

Whitehall, who had come up behind him, was looking over Wild's shoulder at the list of business addresses.

"Want to blow this dump and get a bite to eat?" Wild asked the Teamster. "I hear that little one-arm joint next door ain't bad. All the cops eat there."

13

The mahogany-paneled, marble-floored banquet room on the twelfth floor of the Hollenden Hotel was packed with restless humanity. More than one hundred of the one hundred and twenty-five whose presence had been requested by Chamber of Commerce president Frank Darby had shown up for the afternoon meeting, which had been given the vaguely compelling title, "Cleveland's Brighter Business Tomorrow: A Plan of Action."

The businessmen, seated in chairs facing the riser on which a lectern awaited a speaker, had no notion of the real reason for the gathering. Cigar and cigarette smoke and impatient murmuring mingled in the air.

Eliot Ness, the man who had unbeknownst to them called this meeting, was late.

He had been caught going out the door of his office by a phone call. But that phone call had been important enough to risk the annoyance of the captive audience that awaited him a few blocks away.

"Eliot," the voice said, "how is Cleveland treating you?"

"Fine, Elmer," Ness said, sitting back down at his rolltop desk. "Are you calling from Washington?"

Elmer Irey was the chief of the Special Intelligence Unit of the Internal Revenue Service. Irey had been the Treasury Department counterpart of Justice Department agent Ness in the two-pronged federal assault on Al Capone.

"I am calling from Washington," Irey said. "I'm not out in the field much these days, I'm afraid."

"I doubt they can keep you behind a desk for long."

118

"Well . . ." Irey trailed off.

Irey was a modest, soft-spoken, genuinely nice man; but Ness had a somewhat awkward, strained relationship with him. This stemmed from two things: Ness and his "untouchables" had gotten much more press attention in the Capone bust than their IRS allies; and Ness had let Irey know he didn't approve of the Treasury Department going along with a plea bargain for Capone, which to the embarrassment of Irey and others was rejected derisively by the judge in the case.

"Were you able to check out those returns for me, Elmer? I know I'm trying to do a bit of an end run by coming to you . . ."

"Nonsense. We've helped each other before, and I trust we'll help each other again. Although I'm afraid I may not have been of much help, in this instance. Both Mr. Caldwell and Mr. McFate would appear to be law-abiding citizens, at least as regards their taxes. They file returns—on six-figure incomes, I might add—and pay their Uncle Sam his due."

"They do a lot of cash business. Payoffs under viaducts, back-alley bribes, that kind of thing."

"Well," Irey sighed, "we might well turn that up in a full investigation. And I would certainly take it seriously if you felt such an investigation was worth my unit's time. But I don't have to tell you the difficulty of tracing such transactions."

"No," Ness said, trying to keep his disappointment, his weariness, out of his voice. "You certainly don't. And I'm afraid the job you did on the Capones and Guzik and Nitti, in Chicago, have taught a lot of these hoodlums that the tax laws are the ones they best not break."

"I wish I could be of more help."

"It's generous of you to bend the rules like this, Elmer, in any case."

"Well, there was one item of possible interest."

That perked Ness back up. "Yes?"

"A good share of Caldwell's income is derived from a company called Acme Brothers Glass Works."

Ness scribbled the name on a notepad. "What do you mean 'derived,' exactly?"

"Well, it's his company. He owns it."

Rushing out of the office, heading over to the Hollenden on foot, Ness turned to Captain Savage of the Vandal Squard, who was accompanying him to the meeting, and said, "Ever hear of the Acme Brothers Glass Works?"

"Sure," Savage said, and filled him in.

Minutes later Ness was entering the back of the banquet room, looking across the sea of heads to the dais, where Frank Darby, small and bald and ardent, was patting the air and saying, "Our speaker will be here momentarily, gentlemen . . . your patience, please!"

Ness caught Darby's eye, and Darby smiled and took a seat on the small stage while Ness moved up the center aisle. As people saw who their speaker on "Cleveland's Better Business Tomorrow" actually was, a wave of discontent moved quickly across the room.

Ness took the stage but did not stand behind the lectern. He raised a hand in a stop motion, as if trying to hold back the tide of irritation.

"I'm sure you all feel taken advantage of," Ness said, "by Mr. Darby and myself. Many of you have spoken either to me, or to members of my staff, about the labor racketeering problem in Cleveland, as it applies to you individually and collectively. And all of you, to a man, have sent me and my men packing."

Seated about midway in the room, Vernon Gordon stood. He was white with anger. "I am a busy man, Mr. Ness. We are all busy men. We've every one of us told you how we feel about this matter."

Smiling gently, Ness shook his head. "No you haven't, Vern. You haven't begun to tell me how you feel. You've told me what you've decided to do for the sake of expediency. For the sake of business."

Gordon spoke through his teeth; he wore indignation like a second skin. "The taxpayers don't pay *our* salaries, Mr. Ness. We are in business. We have to be open for business, every day. You make it sound like we're doing something wrong, by trying to keep our businesses open and thriving."

Ness looked hard at the man. "You *are* doing something wrong. You're in tacit collusion with these venal bastards. And you damn well know it, Vern."

"I don't have to listen to this," Gordon said, and began to edge his way out to the aisle.

"I said you haven't told me how you *feel* about the labor racketeering problem. But I know how you feel, Vern—you and every man in this room. You're mad as hell that you have to deal with these bastards. You're mad as hell with yourselves for giving in to them."

Gordon halted in the aisle; he turned and looked at Ness and said, "Just what would you suggest we do?"

Ness spread his arms, opened his hands. "Look around you. Look how many of you there are. Look at how many of the most successful—I would even say powerful—men in this city are sitting in this room. And this group, this successful, powerful group, is letting itself be pushed around by two petty hoodlums. Just because it's easier to pay 'em off than stand up to them."

Gordon's arms were at his side. "You want us to testify."

"You're goddamn right I want you to testify."

Silence hung in the room.

Then Gordon said, "Eliot, do you know what you're asking? I was almost killed." He turned and looked around, saying to his fellow businessmen, "Do you know what it's like to duck a damn tommy gun?"

"Yes," Ness said.

There were some smiles in the audience.

Then Gordon turned back to Ness, and had to smile a little. He said sheepishly, "That was meant to be a rhetorical question."

"Vern. Find a seat. Hear me out."

Gordon sighed, shook his head, and with an air of resignation moved back down the row to his seat; but he sat with arms crossed and the expression of one who would be hard to sell.

A man stood in the back row.

"Mr. Ness," he said, "my name's Wilson—I have a shoe store on Euclid. I frankly don't know why I was invited here today. I paid a certain amount of tribute to Big Jim and Little Jim when I remodeled recently. I considered that a business expense. But when they came around wanting more, wanting me to kick in to this so-called window washers union, I drew the line. I told 'em to go fuh—Well, it's a physical impossibility, but I encouraged 'em to give it the old college try."

There were more smiles, and some nods. Others in the room had shared similar experiences.

"Some of you," Ness said, reaching in his inside coat pocket and withdrawing several folded, stapled sheets, "are here because you are on this list."

Like something choreographed for a Busby Berkley movie musical, every man in the audience sat forward, interested, alert.

"I should say, blacklist. I have obtained a copy of this infamous, legendary document, and it includes a good number of you, gentlemen. Some of you have been marked for vandalism that has not yet occurred. I would venture to say, Mr. Wilson, that your store windows will not last the month out. Others of you are not to be sold glass under any circumstances. Right now your windows are boarded up, and will stay that way, until you pay tribute to the two Jims—if they have their way, that is. This list has been circulated to every glass company in the city."

He nodded to Captain Savage, who began to pass out copies, one per row.

" A few copies of the list are being handed out among you now," Ness said. "Have a quick look, find your name if you like, then pass it along. Don't keep it. We'll be collecting these as you go."

Gordon stood again. "Where did you get that list?"

"I'm not at liberty to say."

"Will it hold up in court?"

"Prosecutor Cullitan tells me it has evidential value, yes."

Gordon's skeptical expression faded as he sat back down, hands on his knees now.

"And today," Ness said, "another interesting piece of information found its way to my office—courtesy of the IRS, a group that probably is not high on any of your personal lists." The remark brought murmurs of mild amusement. "However, I think we owe the Internal Revenue Service a debt of gratitude in this instance. Their records indicate that James Caldwell is the owner of Acme Brothers Glass Works—which Captain Savage tells me has a lock on better than fifty percent of the market in Cleveland. Not only is Caldwell breaking your windows, gentlemen, *and* taking payoffs for allowing union glaziers to replace those broken windows, *and* hitting you up for washing those windows once they've been replaced . . . he's selling you the damn windows. It's his glass."

"And our ass," somebody in back said.

Now there was widespread laughter, but it died out quickly, choking on its own bitterness.

Ness raised a hand and an eyebrow. "Gentlemen, you have heard me, and my staff members, speak of 'safety in numbers.' Look around you. I will promise you now that if I can't find sixty of you to testify, I won't ask any one of you to."

The men began to look at each other, surprised by such an extreme statement.

"This inquiry is a wide-ranging one," Ness said. "I'm already in the process of gathering witnesses from outside the city, specifically businessmen who have been driven from Cleveland because of the tribute these gangsters demand. We will go to the grand jury with an unbeatable case, or we won't go at all. That's my pledge to those of you who are willing to get involved."

Gordon stood again; this time he seemed almost embarrassed. "Eliot, much of what you say makes sense. You're making a convincing case, I admit that. But I have a family. We're many of us, most of us, family men."

"And you're testifying against gangsters," Ness said, nodding. "Your concerns are well-founded. But I promise you we will maintain strict secrecy as to the identities of the witnesses when the case goes to the grand jury. We'll allow no newspaper pictures taken in the courtroom. And we'll post police details at the homes of witnesses, making every effort to provide the maximum of protection."

Gordon sat back down, slowly.

"I don't want any of you to tell me today, at this meeting, what you've decided. In order to maintain secrecy, we'll contact you individually. It was not my intention, today, to gather all of you together to put you on the spot."

That eased the tension in the air, somewhat. And Ness could sense that he'd won, or was winning. He could see it in the faces. In the eyes.

"The Cleveland experience with labor racketeering in recent years," Ness said, "has been costly indeed. Construction has been choked. Building costs have soared. Vandalism has cost businessmen like yourselves, not to mention the public, thousands upon thousands of dollars. It has to stop. You have to stop it, gentlemen."

A man off to the left stood. Ness recognized him as Oscar Reynolds, who ran a men's clothing shop in the Old Arcade.

"No offense, Mr. Ness," Reynolds said, "but aren't you making this out to be something rather larger than it is? This is a small-time extortion racket, not Al Capone."

Ness smiled knowingly. "Al Capone, or what he has come to represent, is exactly what this is. I am convinced that the labor racketeering in this city is tied into the national network of organized crime. The bootlegging gangsters who were orphaned by Repeal, gentlemen, quickly found other things to do with their talents . . . and breaking your windows, and charging you for the privilege, is one of them."

He let that sink in for a moment, then he said, "Thank you for your time," and quickly stepped down from the podium and left the room, even as Captain Savage was collecting the copies of the blacklist.

14

Jack Whitehall took two pork chops off the platter and passed it to dinner guest Sam Wild. Whitehall's wife Sarah, in her blue-and-white print dress and white apron, finally took a seat in the small, blindingly white kitchen. Their two girls—Jane, six, and Dorrie, four—had eaten earlier and were in the living room, playing dolls.

"Delicious, Mrs. Whitehall," Wild said. For a skinny guy, he was putting the food away pretty good.

Both men wore suits and ties and, despite eating in the kitchen, there was an air of formality about the occasion.

"Thank you, Mr. Wild," Sarah said. And she smiled shyly and took a bite of her homemade applesauce.

Whitehall loved his wife very much; she was as attractive as the day he met her, back in Chicago, some ten years before. But her quiet femininity masked a streak of bad temper, as Whitehall well knew. When he stepped out on her, during her first pregnancy, and she found out about it, she had come at him with a rolling pin. Just like Maggie in "Bringing Up Father," only it didn't strike him as funny: it just struck him.

Hell, he wouldn't have her any other way. He liked her quiet manner, but he also liked her passion. He had never stepped out on her since, and swore to himself he never would again. He loved her too goddamn much, and besides, who needed another skull fracture?

125

"These pork chops are to die for," Wild said, patting his face with a napkin.

Sarah smiled shyly.

"Of course," the reporter said slyly, "I always suspected you were an unrepentant pork-chopper, Jack."

A "pork-chopper" was, of course, a fat-salaried, do-nothing union official.

Whitehall smiled thinly. "Nobody ever called me that to my face before, Sam—even jokingly. Nobody ever felt they knew me well enough to."

Wild glanced up from his food, a nervous look flickering across his features. "Hey, I was just kiddin' around."

Then Whitehall laughed and said, "Don't believe everything you hear about me, Sam. My reputation as a roughneck is exaggerated."

Wild raised an eyebrow. "Well, you make the papers often enough."

"Don't believe everything you read in the papers, Sam."

"You're tellin' me?"

"Labor organizers are to a man supposed to be muscle-bound, cigar-smoking slobs who get fat and cocky by stealing hard-earned dues out of the pockets of the overworked proletariat."

Wild glanced at Whitehall's wife, obviously choosing his words carefully so as not to offend her. Then he returned his gaze to his host and said, "Jack, you can't tell me that you haven't . . . leaned on people, from time to time?"

Whitehall shrugged. "It's a class struggle. And no class struggle is without its"—now Whitehall chose his words carefully—"physical aspects."

Wild began to say something, then glanced at Mrs. Whitehall again, grinned wryly and returned to his pork chops.

After dessert (pecan pie with ice cream), Whitehall and Wild withdrew to the front porch to have a smoke. They sat on the swing. Whitehall was about to roll a Bull

Durham, but Wild stopped him, handing him a fat, fancy cigar.

"Don't worry about reinforcing the stereotype, Mr. Whitehall," Wild said with arch formality, lighting a wooden match off a post and helping Whitehall get the cigar going. "I ain't about to write you off as a muscle-bound, cigar-smoking slob."

Whitehall drew in on the cigar, relishing it; it was as rich as the lining of a millionaire's smoking jacket. "I thought you were a Lucky Strike man, Wild."

"Oh I am," Wild said, smirking as he lit up his own fat stogie. "But I thought we oughta enjoy these Havanas together. After all, I got 'em out of Caldwell's office the other night."

Whitehall had a good laugh over that, and Wild joined in some, and the two big men sat on the porch swing, like a courting couple, swinging and smoking, gently, swinging and smoking.

"Are you and Ness really pals?" Wild asked after a while.

"That's putting it a mite strong. We worked side by side in the Pullman plant in Chicago, for about six months. We got along. He was a smart kid. Hard-working little son of a bitch."

"He hasn't changed much. Sometimes I feel like planting a nice fat cream pie in that S.O.B.'s smug puss."

Whitehall laughed. "I thought you two were friends."

"Yeah, we're friends. But I'd still like to hit the bastard with a pie."

"Well, he did con us into doing his work for him." Whitehall sat and enjoyed the warm, gentle breeze for a few moments; it went well with the Havana. Then he said: "We make an unlikely team, Sam, considering the bullshit your paper's been printing about the Teamsters."

Wild shrugged. "You shouldn't have passed that motion barring the press from your meetings."

Whitehall didn't push it; nor did Wild. They sat in silence, listening to the noises of the neighborhood, the muffled sound of radios, the clinking of dishes being washed and dried, the traffic of the nearby main thorough-fare.

"I don't know whether I'm supposed to tell you this or not," Wild said.

"You want me to get some whiskey, to help you decide?"

"Yeah. Why don't you?"

Whitehall went in and got a bottle and two glasses and returned. He poured Wild, and then himself, a drink.

"Anyway," Wild said, "you have a right to know, although by all rights it should be Ness who tells you."

"Tell me."

"Then again, he might not tell you. Might not want you told."

"You tell me. We put our butts on the line."

Wild thought about that. Then he raised his glass to Whitehall and Whitehall raised his and they clinked glasses in a toast to their teamwork.

"Vernon Gordon came forward," Wild revealed.

"Damn. That's good news."

"You're goddamn right it's good news. Gordon was the key witness, the one guy Ness felt he *had* to get in front of the grand jury. I mean, Gordon suffered the most outrageous vandalism of anybody. Machine fuckin' gun, no less."

Whitehall raised a hand. "Keep it down, please. Better watch the language. My kids are right inside."

Wild made an apologetic face and gesture, and went on. "Ness spoke to a whole group of them, a hundred or more of the businessmen that the two Jims have been preying on; and he told them he wouldn't ask any of them to testify unless there was a total of sixty witnesses that came forward."

"So how many came forward?"

Wild smiled. "Sixty-one."

"Ha. Just made it."

"Any number of 'em, including Gordon, said they'd testify in any case."

"How did Ness pull that off, anyway?"

Wild grimaced. "I don't know how he pulls off half of what he pulls off. But he's got a good share of the business community behind him."

Whitehall sipped his whiskey, nodding. "That's what worries me about my old co-worker."

"What?"

"I'm afraid he's gonna wind up in the pocket of those 'prominent businessmen' and 'captains of industry' and 'social leaders' he hangs out with at the country club and so on. Hell, he lives in a damn boathouse that belongs to Wynston, who's got dough in Fisher Body, for crying out loud."

Wild was slowly nodding. "I know. I been telling him that. But he doesn't want to listen. Eliot Ness likes to think that those guys are civic-minded and that all they'll ask of him is to do his job and do it well. Which he does in spades, obviously."

Whitehall shook his head. "It won't be that simple. The bill will come due. Again and again."

Wild shrugged. "What can I say? I agree with you."

They sat in silence, drinking and smoking.

Finally, Wild stood and said, "I got work to do. And it's getting late."

Whitehall rose. "Thanks for coming."

"Thanks for the invite."

The two men shook hands, smiling at each other with cigars stuck in their smiles.

Then Whitehall accompanied Wild back inside, where the reporter thanked Sarah again and said his good-byes to her and the kids.

Once Wild had been seen off, Whitehall removed his suitcoat and his tie and shoes; he put on his bedroom slippers and padded into the girls' room, where Sarah, in her dressing gown, was reading them *The Wizard of Oz*. He sat on the edge of the bed, stroking Dorrie's hair, listening to the gentle, musical sound of his wife's voice.

Both his girls had Sarah's sky-blue eyes. Neither one of
them had a facial feature that resembled their father, a fact
for which he was grateful.

"What did you girls do today?" he asked them, after
his wife had finished tonight's chapter.

The little girls spoke of their day, in overlapping
sentences, none of which made much sense; their concerns were trivial, though so important to them. He
listened to and savored the sound of their voices, and
nodded when it seemed appropriate, without really listening to the words.

He hugged Dorrie and kissed her on the cheek, and
then went around and hugged Janey and kissed her on the
forehead.

"That's what Glinda did," Janey said.

"Huh?" Whitehall said.

"She kissed Dorothy on the forehead. And it protected
her. Nothing could hurt her."

"Nothing," Dorrie said, wide-eyed and nodding.

"That's nice," Whitehall said, and smiled back at
them, loving them without understanding a damn word of
it.

In the hall he hugged Sarah to him; she was so much
smaller than he was, it was like hugging another child.
She beamed up at him, with the same sky-blue eyes as the
kids, and said, "I can kiss you on the forehead, too, if you
like."

"Ha. I don't think that'll do me much good."

"Well then, let me just do this, then."

And she kissed him on the mouth. A sweet kiss that
had more than a hint of passion in it.

Then, with an ornery little smile, she looked up at
him and said, "Are you coming to bed, you big bully?"

"Yeah. After my radio program."

"What, Eddie Cantor, again?"

"He's funny, honey."

She rolled her eyes. "Then to bed?"

"Then to bed."

She turned to go and looked at him with a mock mean

look, as if to say *You better,* and he reached out and patted her on her sweet soft ass and her expression melted and she padded down the hall in bare feet.

In the living room he switched on the radio, dialed his station, and settled himself in his easy chair, waiting for his show to come on. Hands folded in his lap, he felt himself on the verge of drifting off to sleep. The overstuffed chair, next to the porch windows, was as comfortable as a mother's arms. It soothed his weary damn bones. He'd had another long day at the food terminal, though well worthwhile. The Teamsters would have that place sewed up in a week.

Whitehall smiled to himself, pleased with his life. He had come a long, long way from that log cabin on Lake Michigan. He had little memory of his father, who had run a small grocery store at Scott's Point, serving a small community of fishermen and loggers. From the age of six he'd been raised by his grandfather on a small farm, and when his grandfather died, went to live with his foundry-foreman uncle in Manistique, Michigan, a town of five thousand whose electric lights, running water, indoor plumbing, movie house, and department stores had opened up a whole new world for the burly bumpkin.

He had also been introduced to pool halls and street gangs, and with his brawn and brains had little trouble maintaining respect and even dominion. Whitehall was an unusual roughneck among roughnecks, because he studied, and liked to read. He grew up on Zane Grey and Tom Swift and was a reader to this day, everything from Karl Marx to Sinclair Lewis.

Of course, it was the sons and daughters of bankers, merchants, doctors, and lawyers who went to college; and occasionally the offspring of the middle class, the department-store clerks, the bank tellers, the civil-service workers. Not the likes of Jack Whitehall, the ill-clad kin of a foundry worker.

He had hoboed around awhile after high school, and took his first real job on a Great Lakes steamer out of Toledo. Working in the galley as a kitchen flunky, he set tables and washed dishes, pots and pans, and swabbed floors. He'd been forced to sign up in the Lakes Carriers Association, a company union. It had been his first lesson in the education of a working man. When the ship steward, to whom he reported, got sacked for drinking on the job, the steward's three-man staff, hardworking Jack Whitehall included, was canned as well.

Like all company unions, there was no real grievance committee; nothing to protect the worker from unjust firings. It had made an impression on young Whitehall. When he finally wound up in Chicago, in the Pullman plant, working back-breaking twelve-hour shifts, he was a man born to the union cause.

A man with a brain in his head and steel in his fists could go a long way for the worker, and for himself. Yes, he was in it for himself and his family, but he was no goddamn pork-chopper. Yes, he used threats and violence when that was what it took to get the job done. But he sure as hell was no shakedown artist like those bastards Caldwell and McFate, who gave the labor movement the worst kind of bad name. Much as he distrusted and even hated cops, he was glad he'd helped Ness try to nail those bums.

And, knowing that stubborn Scandyhoovian (as Nordics like Ness were called back where Whitehall came from), he would get the job done.

Eddie Cantor came on and woke Whitehall up. Soon he was laughing, as Cantor dueled first with the Mad Russian ("How dooo you dooo?"—that always killed Whitehall) and then with that lovable dope Parkyakarkas.

Despite the radio (which wasn't turned up all that loud, with the kids sleeping in the other room), a noise on the porch caught Whitehall's attention. He turned his head slightly and looked over his shoulder, and through the thin white translucent curtain he could make out the figure of a man holding something.

The window behind him shattered under the chatter of a machine gun and slugs riddled the left side of his body and the back of his neck; he began to rise and more bullets tore into him, tore through him, shaking him like a large animal shakes a smaller one in its teeth, and he fell awkwardly to the floor, tumbling, doing an ungainly little dance, dead before the pain could register, dead before he could see his living room and its nice overstuffed furniture get the stuffing knocked out of it, as bullets chewed up the room, shutting off the radio, cutting off Eddie Cantor in mid-joke, the sound of female screams, a mother and her two girls, cutting shrilly above the metallic din.

15

The body was gone by the time Ness got there; only a chalk outline remained. Both the coroner's man and the photographer were gone as well. Nonetheless, the crime scene was freshly preserved; the murder might have occurred minutes ago, not several hours.

He'd been stuck in an endless, budget-battle city council meeting, seated at Mayor Burton's side, when a plainclothes cop sent by Sergeant Merlo of the Homicide Bureau brought him the news of the Whitehall shooting. With the mayor's permission, Ness had left the meeting. He'd run into Sam Wild coming out of the press room.

"Were your ears burning tonight?" Wild had asked with a one-sided smile.

"Why?" Ness said, moving quickly down the hall, footsteps echoing off the marble floor.

Wild followed along. "I had dinner at Jack Whitehall's tonight. You were a frequent topic of conversation."

Ness looked at him sharply. "When was this?"

"Oh, I don't know. I went over about six-thirty, stayed till eight, maybe."

"Within an hour of your leaving," Ness said, "Jack Whitehall was murdered."

The usually unflappable Wild stopped dead. His face drained of blood.

Ness kept walking, slipping his trench coat on, looking back to say, "Machine-gunned through his front-porch window."

Wild caught up. "His wife and kids . . . ?"

"Unharmed."

"I'm coming along."

"It's not really appropriate, Sam, a reporter at the scene at this stage."

"Fuck you, I'm coming."

"I guess you're coming."

The living room of Whitehall's home was a grisly sight. Next to the white chalk outline on the natural wood floor, which was splashed with blood and brain matter and assorted gore, were hundreds of fragments of glass that had been blown out by the machine-gun fire. The chopper had apparently been thrust right up to the pane. Some of the shards had been scattered across the room; the pattern of slugs was stitched in the wall opposite Whitehall's bullet-tattered easy chair. The radio had taken a dozen slugs easily. The effeminate portrait of Christ still hung on the wall, albeit crookedly now; its glass had been shattered and the Savior had gotten one in the cheek.

Grim as all of this was, Ness was pleased that the evidence had not been disturbed; before his arrival in Cleveland, crime-scene procedure here was unprofessional, to say the least. His first move had been to remind his detectives of the "golden rule" for investigators as stated by Hans Gross in *System der Kriminalistik* back in 1906: "Never alter the position of, pick up, or even touch any object before it has been minutely described in an official note and a photograph taken."

The efficiency of this crime-scene investigation was due, Ness knew, to the man in charge, Sergeant Martin Merlo, the somber, professorial detective whose primary ongoing assignment was the Mad Butcher of Kingsbury Run case. Two other detectives were present as well, one of them notating a crime-scene floor plan on a clipboard, the other making detailed field notes in a small notebook. And several uniformed officers were posted at the street and in back of the house, keeping out the curious.

"You know Sam Wild," Ness said, gesturing behind him with one hand, taking off his fedora with the other.

"Yes," Merlo said indifferently, aware that the safety

director cut a lot of slack to the press in general and Wild in particular.

"Where's Mrs. Whitehall?"

"She's in the bedroom," Merlo said. He was a thin middle-aged man with horn-rimmed glasses. "There's a doctor with her, a fellow who lives a few doors down. They sent for him even before they called the police."

"And the children?"

"Whitehall has a brother in town. He and his wife came over and picked the kids up and are taking care of them." Merlo made a clicking sound in his cheek. "Poor kids looked awful—not crying, just stunned, white as little ghosts."

"Give me a reading of the situation."

"Well, we have a witness."

"Good."

"But not much of one."

"Oh?" Ness's eyes were fixed on the chalk outline on the floor; the outline looked ridiculously large, but then, Whitehall had been a big man.

"Fellow who lives upstairs," Merlo explained. "He has a wife and a teenage daughter, but they were at the movies tonight. He heard the shots, looked out the window, and saw a figure running toward the street, getting in a car parked in front of the Whitehall house. The car drove north on East Boulevard."

"Did he get a look at the guy?"

"No. No physical description except a big man in a raincoat, collar up."

"License plate number?"

"No."

"Did he describe the car?"

"A dark sedan."

"That's it? No make? No color?"

"No. You might want to talk to him yourself."

Ness sighed. "And the neighbors on either side?"

"Nothing. They heard the noise, of course. They say they thought it was a car backfiring."

Ness looked at Wild, who rolled his eyes.

"That's one way of not getting involved," Ness said

glumly. "Well, you've done a good job of preserving the crime scene, Sergeant."

"Thanks. We staked off the front yard; ground's a little damp from that rain yesterday, but I don't think we're going to find any footprints. The gunman came up the front walk, onto the porch, and fired a volley through the window there. Then he went back the way he came."

Ness had a closer look, stepping carefully around the chalk outline and squeezing next to the easy chair, which angled away from the southernmost of four windows looking out on the porch. Blood was spattered on the teeth of glass remaining in the window. Strands of Whitehall's hair clung to the sheer curtains.

"Ballistics make an I.D. yet?" Ness asked.

"Cowley is still here; he's got a big job, with all these slugs. Want to talk to him?"

"Yes."

Leaving Merlo and Wild inside, Ness found Cowley, a plump, pleasant man of about thirty-five with reddish-blond, thinning hair, on the porch using a tape measure to pinpoint the location of the various shell casings. He was making field notes and then picking up each shell casing with the pencil he was taking notes with, before dropping each casing into small, individual manila evidence envelopes. It was a tedious process, but Cowley didn't seem to mind. One of the top ballistics experts on the department, Cowley had been handpicked by Ness himself.

"David," Ness said. "What do we have here?"

Cowley stood, smiled a greeting, holding up a cartridge casing on his pencil. "Forty-five caliber. Machine gun—look at the number of casings, and the direction and the force with which they've been ejected. Judging by the pattern of the breech face marks on the cartridge, the firing-pin marks, the characteristic bulge of the cartridge, I'd say probably a Thompson."

"Only one weapon?"

"So far that's all I've identified. Wasn't one weapon enough?"

Ness pointed at the cartridge riding the pencil. "I

want you to compare those to the casings from the Gordon's restaurant shooting."

"Fine," Cowley said, nodding. "Any connection besides machine guns used in both?"

"You tell me."

Cowley nodded. "I won't get to it till tomorrow. I'm going to be here awhile."

Ness nodded. He well knew that Cowley had hours ahead of him here. When the ballistics man was finished on the porch, he would have to move inside and begin dealing with the spent bullets in the walls and elsewhere. Each slug would have to be removed from its point of impact, the location of which would have to be logged; this procedure, too, was tedious, as care had to be taken so that the cutting instrument Cowley used did not ruin identifying characteristics on the soft metal of the spent bullets.

Ness went back inside, about to join Merlo and Wild in conversation, when a somber man about fifty, in shirtsleeves, pushing up his wire-framed glasses on his sweaty brow, came out from the hallway that led to the bedrooms.

"Is Mr. Ness here?" the man said.

"I'm Ness."

"Mrs. Whitehall would like to see you."

"And you are?"

"Dr. Spencer. I'm the family doctor."

Ness nodded and walked toward the hall, but the doctor touched him on the arm, halting him. With a tortured expression, the doctor said, "She's insisting, but don't stay long. She's really very upset."

"Understandably."

"I'd like to sedate her, but she won't allow it until she's talked to you."

Ness nodded again.

Mrs. Whitehall, her pretty face devoid of makeup, her complexion white, her eyes red, sat up in the bed, covers at her waist. She had an oddly blank look.

"Close the door, Mr. Ness."

Ness did.

He stood at her bedside. "I'm dreadfully sorry for—"

She raised a hand in a stop motion. She was staring straight ahead, into the darkness at the edges of the barely lit room.

"He was so gentle tonight," she said. "Tucking the girls in. Kissing them good night."

Ness said nothing.

She looked up at him. Her eyes were wide and hollow. "Jack was doing something for you, wasn't he?"

Ness hesitated for a moment, then nodded.

"Helping you."

"Yes."

"You were his friend."

"I liked Jack. I respected him. He was the best man in his world."

She smiled bitterly. "Did you get him killed?"

The words hit Ness like a blow.

Swallowing, he said, "I don't know."

"Don't you?"

"I may have," Ness admitted.

The bitter smile began to tremble. Tears began to slide down the white cheeks. "Are you satisfied with . . . with the result?"

"Mrs. Whitehall, I . . . I don't know what to say. I can only assure you that the person who did this—actually, the persons, I think the man who fired the weapon was only a weapon of sorts himself—will be tracked down. I will give this my personal attention, I promise you."

"That is so big of you, Mr. Ness. So very big."

"I understand your bitterness, Mrs. Whitehall. I know that finding Jack's killers won't bring him back. But it's about all I can offer."

She reached out and up and slapped his face.

The sound was ringing. The pain was sharp.

"Get out," she said.

Ness nodded and went out.

Merlo was conferring with one of his detectives. Ness stopped and waited till the exchange was over, then spoke to the detective in charge.

"I want you to work with Albert Curry on this," Ness said. "You've worked together before, and well."

"Yes, we have," Merlo said, with a gentle smile, "on several occasions. But tell me . . . why is the safety director involving a member of his personal staff in a murder investigation? Frankly, I think the Detective Bureau is quite capable of—"

"Of course. Particularly with you on the job, Sergeant. But this is, obviously, a labor-related killing. And my office is involved in an ongoing wide-ranging inquiry into labor racketeering."

"Ah, yes. Of course. So I need to keep Captain Savage of the Vandal Squad informed as well."

"He and his men are assigned directly to me now."

"This labor inquiry is a major effort you're making, then."

There was a faint tone of disapproval in Merlo's voice, and Ness knew why: Merlo was still irritated that the full-scale investigation of the Kingsbury Run mass murderer, in which Ness and his staff had been closely involved, had been cut back to just Merlo himself.

"Martin," Ness said, putting a hand on the detective's shoulder, "I'm in your corner where Kingsbury Run is concerned. But the mayor pulled me and my staff off that case. We both know the Butcher will eventually resurface and we'll be back in business."

"But it will take another killing to do that. We should be trying to find the bastard, to stop him before he kills again."

"You're still on that case, Sergeant. But you're also on this one. And I expect your full attention."

"You'll get it." There was resignation, but no resentment, in Merlo's tone.

"I know I will."

"And," Merlo said, looking around the bullet-torn room, "this won't be a picnic. Whitehall had a lot of enemies. He's been the business agent for the Ice, Coal, and Water Wagon Drivers Union for seven years, and during that time he's been in conflict with all sorts and classes of people."

"True."

"A man like that, who used his fists so frequently, who used his size to bulldoze so many people . . . literally hundreds of industrials hated him. Some probably enough to kill him."

"One did, at least."

"He was suspected of bombing that coal-company office a couple of years ago. He did time in the workhouse for an assault charge and malicious property damage, in another matter, and had an assault charge coming up for a police officer he roughed up."

"I know all that."

"Do you. According to your reporter friend, you were a friend of Whitehall's."

"We were friendly acquaintances."

The eyes behind the horn rims were shrewd and narrow. "Is there anything else you'd care to tell me about this case, Mr. Ness? Such as what brought you to the scene?"

Ness smiled, even though his cheek still stung.

"You're a good detective, Sergeant. Great instincts. Let's step outside."

They did. They moved off the porch, away from Cowley, who was still kneeling at the altar of ejected shell casings. They stood on the sidewalk. Past the roped-off front yard, Wild was out having a smoke, his cigarette an amber eye in the night.

Ness said, "Whitehall was doing some poking around for me."

"What sort?"

"Into labor matters. Specifically involving Big Jim Caldwell and Little Jim McFate."

"I see."

Ness filled Merlo in, in more detail, alluding to the acquisition of the blacklist by Whitehall without quite spelling it out, without mentioning Wild's role at all.

"This is helpful background," Merlo said. "What was Whitehall working on lately, do you know?"

"He was organizing the food terminal, in the wake of

our ouster of Harry Gibson, who was Big Jim and Little Jim's man. Hey! That's a thought..."

"What is?"

"There was a machine-gunning of a farmer's vehicle at the food market. Sort of a grand-gesture scare tactic, not unlike the Gordon's restaurant shooting. Gibson himself did it, apparently, though we never could quite get a witness to swear to that."

"Maybe Gibson did the Gordon's shooting."

Ness poked Merlo knowingly in the chest. "Maybe he did this one, too."

"Do we have shell casings or spent slugs or anything from the food-terminal shooting? If we could match 'em with what we have here..."

Ness sighed. "Unfortunately, no. Vandalism sites aren't generally treated as crime scenes. I checked on that already, after what happened at Gordon's."

"But do we have any casings or slugs from Gordon's? Was *that* treated as a crime scene?"

"It wasn't," Ness said, "but I picked up casings and slugs myself, there."

Merlo smiled and nodded. "You're a good detective, Mr. Ness. Great instincts."

The two men smiled at each other, a bit awkwardly, and Ness said, "You take it from here, Sergeant. We'll talk tomorrow."

"Yes we will," Merlo said, and headed back inside.

Ness joined Wild on the sidewalk.

"What did Mrs. Whitehall want?" the reporter asked, pitching a spent Lucky Strike into the darkness.

"To slap me."

"Oh, Christ. I'm sorry, Eliot."

"Maybe I had it coming. Maybe I got her husband killed."

"Bullshit. That idealistic roughneck knew exactly what risks he was taking, and why."

Ness sighed. "You may be right."

"You know I'm right. Besides, I don't think his working for you is necessarily what got him killed."

"Oh?"

"Who knew about it but the three of us?"

"We can't know if Jack kept it to himself."

"I'd bet my ass on him keeping it to himself. Who the hell in his circles could he tell he was in bed with the likes of you? Cops are poison to guys like Whitehall. They'd've thrown him out of his union post if they knew he was keeping company as lousy as you."

Ness managed to smile a little. "You know how to build up a fella's confidence."

"Well, it's true. But I think Big Jim and Little Jim *were* behind it, just the same."

Ness nodded. "Because Jack was organizing the food terminal. Because he was stepping in and taking over while they were indisposed."

"Exactly."

"Well, that's just another way it's my fault, Sam. I opened that door for Jack."

"Well what in the hell do you intend to do about it?"

"What I told his widow I'd do. Find the sons of bitches responsible."

Wild snorted. "Well, you know who that is."

"Yeah. The two Jims. And I'd bet a year's pay that Harry Gibson, their out-of-work one-man goon squad from the food terminal, is wielding that tommy gun for 'em."

Wild lit up another Lucky. "Jack Whitehall would probably have taken a baseball bat and beat their brains out. Or blown 'em up with a bomb or something. What will you do?"

"All I can do is put them in jail," Ness said, digging, his hands in his topcoat pockets. "Or hope they resist arrest when I come to pick them up."

"So you have a reason to kill them?"

Ness smiled faintly. "I already have a reason," he said. "It's an excuse I'm looking for."

TWO

November 7–December 20, 1937

16

Just a few months ago he had been in another funeral home, in Cleveland, at the wake of Jack Whitehall. He hadn't been able to stay long—Whitehall's widow remained bitter toward him—but he'd paid his respects. Said good-bye to an old friend, an old co-worker.

Now, on this dreary Sunday afternoon, Eliot Ness was in Chicago, in Doty's funeral home on 115th Street, back in his old Roseland neighborhood, just a few blocks from the frame house where he'd been raised. He was saying good-bye to his mother, dead of a heart attack at seventy-three; five years ago, his father had gone the same way.

But he was also saying good-bye to Roseland. Driving over here from the lavishly lawned Hotel Florence, across from the Pullman plant where he'd worked, going past Palmer Park where he'd played, he felt tugs from his past, felt his last real tie with his youth slip away. He would never live here again. He would rarely visit—only his schoolteacher sister Effie still lived in Roseland; his other two sisters, Clara and Nora, and his brother Charles, had all moved away. The family business, his father's bakery, had been sold years ago.

Effie was the only one of his siblings present in the long, narrow parlor, a very Protestant room, with its dark wood and small stained-glass windows. His brother and his other two sisters would be coming in by train later today. Now, suffering the too-sweet smell of funereal flowers, he stood making meaningless conversation with faces both familiar and foreign, reaching into his memory for the

names of these men and women his age who had stayed in
Roseland. The men, most of them, worked in the Pullman
plant where Ness had briefly toiled as a young man,
dipping radiators. The women looked much older than
they should, with lined faces and clinging children. Among
the older folks paying their respects was the now-retired
Pullman office manager who had told Ness's mother that
her son could always count on a job anytime he wanted it.

That had made his mother proud. She'd been a little
too proud of him, he was afraid; not so long ago she had
given an embarrassing interview to Sam Wild, damn him,
in which she revealed that her youngest son "was so
terribly good as a boy, he never got a spanking . . . I never
saw a baby like him." Even worse, Sam had coaxed her
into saying that she wasn't the least bit surprised that her
youngest child had "the country's attention focused on his
work on rebuilding a major city's crime prevention and
law enforcement activities."

He'd been surprised that even Sam Wild could whee-
dle such admissions out of Mama ("I always expected Eliot
to do outstanding things"); she was too quiet, too reserved
for such remarks. On the other hand, her high opinion of
him was no secret to him. He knew he was the favorite,
and his sisters and brother didn't even seem to mind; they
had fussed over the freckle-faced baby, too.

He knew that he'd been somewhat spoiled as a child;
ten years younger than his nearest sibling, he'd been
doted over, no denying it. Childhoods didn't come much
better. He and his papa would hop a streetcar and take in
a game at White Sox park; or grab the I.C. to Soldier
Field for a football game. His mother would read aloud to
him, and had taught him to read before he entered
kindergarten. When other kids were reading *Captain
Billy's Whiz Bang,* if they could read at all, young Ness
was consuming Sir Arthur Conan Doyle's Sherlock Holmes
tales and the plays of William Shakespeare.

Nonetheless, his parents had encouraged him to be
independent, and there had been no pressure to go into
the family business. In fact, his mother and father had

urged him to go to college, so he could get a top white collar job; they'd been disappointed, but not disapproving, when he went to work at Pullman instead.

The day he came home with a new suit and suitcase, to tell his mother he had enrolled in the University of Chicago, she had said only, "It's like you to enroll first, then tell us." But there had been no disapproval in that. If anything, the opposite. And his father had only nodded, said, "Good," and gone back to puffing his pipe and reading his evening paper.

Now they were both gone. Actually, his mother was still here—in that coffin, across the room. She truly looked peaceful; like she was sleeping. Yes. But Eliot Ness, who had seen more corpses than the undertaker who ran this place, who had seen bodies riddled with bullets, who had seen stiffs knife-slashed from head to foot, had never seen a dead body that disturbed him more.

Thank God for Ev MacMillan. Without her, he was not sure how he could have gotten through this, at least not without breaking down in front of everybody. Right now she was over looking at the many flowers, reading the small cards of condolence.

Evelyn was a slender brunette, twenty-five, who had first caught his eye half a dozen years ago, when he was still head of the Justice Department prohibition unit in Chicago. He had met her and her family socially (her father was a prominent stockbroker); Ness was still married at the time, and Ev was really just a kid, attending the Art Institute. But she had made an impression on him.

And apparently he had on her, as well.

He and Bob Chamberlin had taken the weekend off to take the train to Ann Arbor for the Michigan-Chicago football game. They had run into Ev and some friends at the stadium Saturday, Ev glowing upon seeing Ness, and the whole crew had gone out for dinner after the game, at the hotel. That evening Ness had gotten word his mother had died that afternoon.

He and Ev had become pretty friendly during the course of the day and the early evening, with some slightly inebriated hand-holding and flirting and such ensuing; but he hardly expected Ev to insist on going back to Chicago with him. But insist she did.

"I'm fine," he'd told her, last night at the Ann Arbor train station. "You don't need to come."

"You're not fine. Your heart is breaking, and I'm here to help you pick up the pieces. No arguments."

He hadn't argued. They got a compartment and he had broken down and cried in her arms; he'd been a little drunk, after all. She had comforted him as he hadn't been comforted since . . . well, since his mother comforted him as a kid, he guessed.

He walked over to her, where she was still reading the little cards on the floral arrangements.

"These are all so lovely," she said. "Your mother had many friends. So many friends."

"She and Papa lived in the neighborhood over fifty years."

"It's quite a tribute, so many flowers."

Ness began to read the small cards. Names began to register. Faces that went with the names floated up from his memory.

"One time," he said reflectively, "a man came in the bakery and asked my father to bake a cake in the shape of an M. The next day the man came back and saw what Papa had made and said, 'No, no, no—I want a *fancy* M.' Papa threw the cake away and gave it another go. The next day the man came back in and was handed my father's masterpiece: an ornate M-shaped cake in a flowery script. 'That's more like it!' the man said. And Papa said, 'Shall I wrap it up?' And the man said, 'No thanks, I'll eat it here!'"

Ev smiled at that, and Ness smiled back at her; he had told the story, a favorite of his, to try to cheer himself and Ev up. But for some reason, now he was having to work even harder at holding back the tears.

"Did you see this floral display?" Ev asked, taking his hand, leading him like a child. "It's really quite elaborate . . ." Then she whispered, "Even if it isn't in the best of taste."

It was a garish display, red and white and blue mums, more appropriate to the winner's circle at a horse race than the parlor of a funeral home. An artist like Ev would naturally find it a little distasteful, but Ness figured it was the thought that counts.

Ev read the card. "This is from 'Frank and the Boys.' Who are Frank and the Boys?"

"Let me see that," Ness snapped, and he grabbed the card, pulling it off the tiny string that held it on. Ev was startled, staring wide-eyed as Ness read the card to himself.

He looked at her sharply. "This is from Frank Nitti."

"Oh. Oh my."

"The Chicago Outfit," Ness said bitterly, "paying their respects."

He grabbed the garish wreath and said, "I'll be back."

He marched straight to the rear door and went out into the alley, where a row of one-story parking garages serving adjacent apartment buildings faced the backs of the funeral home and other commercial buildings. Ness carried the wreath to a group of garbage cans behind the store next door and began to beat the wreath against the brick wall savagely, ripping the decorative ribbon, pulverizing the flowers, mashing them to nothing, the wire framework bending, distorting.

When he was finished, he dropped the remains of the wreath into the nearest of the trash cans. Then he stood, with hands balled to fists, and breathed heavily, red with anger.

"Remind me never to send you flowers," a voice said.

Ness turned.

The man standing in the alley, having just come out of the rear door of the funeral home, was a solid six feet tall, with reddish brown hair; his smile was wry but not unkind. His suit was dark and so was his tie. His name was Nathan Heller, and he was an ex-cop pal from Ness's prohibition-unit days; working as a private op out of his own small office, now.

Ness sighed and managed an embarrassed smile.

"Frank Nitti sent those flowers. I guess it must've rubbed me the wrong way."

Heller shrugged. "Maybe Frank didn't mean it as a dig. He respects you."

"I don't respect him. I think he meant it as an insult, and if he didn't, it's an intrusion into my personal life that I damn well don't appreciate."

Heller walked up to Ness and put a hand on his shoulder. "It's good to see you, too, Eliot. Wish it wasn't this way, though."

Ness patted his friend's hand. "Yeah. I know. Thanks for coming."

Heller moved a few steps away. "I didn't know your mom very well. But I do know she raised a hell of a son."

"Thanks."

"Where *is* Charles?"

Ness laughed. "I'm glad you came. We needed to talk, anyway."

"That can wait. Business can wait. We can talk tomorrow."

"No. Let's take some time now. I don't want to go back in there just yet."

Ness put lids on two of the garbage cans, and the two men sat down on them.

"Well, I did finish that job you contracted," Heller said. "In fact, your friend Caldwell headed back to Cleveland just this morning, by train."

Ness had hired Heller, by phone, to shadow Big Jim Caldwell, who had taken a trip to Chicago for a union convention late last week.

"Caldwell met with Louis Campagna at the Bismarck Hotel," Heller said. "They had lunch yesterday. Then they went upstairs."

"To see Nitti?"

"That I'm not sure of. Nitti is known to rent out a suite there, from time to time. But what the hell—Campagna is Nitti's top lieutenant. What more do you need?"

"Nothing more," Ness said.

"Your suspicions were correct, I'd say," the private

detective said. "What's going on in Cleveland is *not* strictly a local deal. It's definitely part of a move by the mob to move in on unions nationally."

"The Chicago mob."

"Well...more than just the Outfit, would be my guess. The whole national syndicate's in this effort."

Ness was nodding. "Thanks, Nate. This will help."

"Where does your investigation stand, anyway?"

"We're in good shape, on the labor racketeering charges. We've got seventy-some witnesses in Cleveland, and I've been gathering more from the midwest and east coast as well. I'm going to follow up on several potential witnesses in Chicago while I'm here in town."

"What about the murder charge? That Whitehall killing?"

Ness shook his head. "We think we know who the shooter was—a strong-arm named Gibson. And we managed to match up the bullets from the Gordon's restaurant shooting to the ones that ripped Jack Whitehall apart."

"Same gun? No question?"

"Same gun. No question. The frustrating thing is, Gibson used a machine gun in a previous vandalism, at the food terminal, but nobody bothered to collect any of the spent slugs as evidence."

Heller shrugged. "It was just a case of vandalism, after all."

"Bullshit. When a machine gun is used, it goes way the hell beyond vandalism. That was sloppy police work, and I blame myself for it."

"You can't be everywhere."

"Perhaps not. But if I had been on top of that one, if I'd seen to it that we treated that food-market machine-gunning as a crime scene, and matched up all three sets of slugs, we'd have Gibson by the short hair."

"And if you could get Gibson, you could probably swap him a life sentence for testimony against Caldwell and McFate."

"Don't I know it. We had him under twenty-four-hour surveillance for a month, but he stayed clean."

Heller slapped the air. "Look, put 'em all away on the racketeering charges. You're gonna have plenty of evidence. Don't be greedy."

Ness smiled. "Look who's talking. The guy who's charging the city of Cleveland thirty-five a day."

"It's my special rate."

"It's your top rate."

"You wouldn't want anything but the best. Besides, you still got that slush fund to dip into, don't you?"

"Yes," Ness said, shaking his head no, "but it's not bottomless. That's a pool I can hit my head on the bottom of, if I take too high a dive."

Heller smirked. "Well. You know my opinion."

"And what is your opinion?"

"Those businessmen who're funding you are at some point going to want something for their money. And I don't mean a safer Cleveland."

Ness laughed shortly. "You and Sam Wild are sure cut out of the same cloth."

"Are you comparing me with that sleazy reporter pal of yours? Why, we got nothin' in common, except one poor misguided friend."

Ness smiled and climbed off the garbage can. "I better get back inside."

"Yeah. You better. I'll go in with you. What time's the memorial service tomorrow?"

"Two-thirty. You don't have to come, Nate. This was more than enough."

"I'll be there. When are you heading back to Cleveland?"

"I don't know. Wednesday, maybe. Maybe Thursday."

"If you're still in town Wednesday, I'll buy you lunch at the Berghoff."

"It's a deal," Ness said. "With the kind of money you're making off the city of Cleveland, you can afford it."

They went back inside.

Heller whispered, "Isn't that Ev MacMillan, the book illustrator?"

"Yeah."

"She's a doll. Is that a case you're working on?"

"Yes it is. Hands off, Heller."

"Just asking. Besides, do I look like a guy who'd come on to a dame in a funeral home?"

"Yes."

Soon Heller was having a conversation with several Chicago cops who had dropped by to pay their respects (the Wentworth District Station was two doors down), and Ness walked out onto the wide, shallow outer parlor where some of the mourners were smoking and lounging in the comfortable leather chairs. Ev was sitting, having a cigarette, taking a break from making conversation with strangers.

He sat next to her. "How are you holding up?"

"Fine. I'm sorry about that business with the wreath . . . I guess I should have recognized what 'Frank and the Boys' referred to."

"No you shouldn't. Forget it."

"I hope you don't mind my sending that friend of yours back out there to see you."

"So you've met Heller?"

"Not really. He's a nice-looking man. What's the story on him?"

"He used to be a cop. A plainclothes dick on the pickpocket squad. He was one of the few relatively honest cops I could count on as a reliable contact."

"What is he up to now?"

"He got into some political trouble on the force, and quit. The corruption was getting to him. He's more honest than he likes to think."

She smiled knowingly, nodding. "At a time like this, it's nice to have a friend like that."

He held her hand. "Yes it is. You know, you don't have to hang around here if you—"

"Shush. Are you going to stay at the hotel again tonight?"

"Well, I was planning to. If I stayed with Effie and her husband, the only bed available—"

"Is your mother's."

He swallowed. "Yes."

"I have an apartment on the North Side, you know."

"Don't you have a roommate?"

"No. But I'd like to have one. Tonight."

"This is . . ."

"So sudden? Eliot, I like you. And I think you need somebody at your side, right now. We don't have to be anything but friends."

He squeezed her hand. "Oh yes we do."

She touched his face with a smooth, cool hand. "It's going to be fine. It's going to be fine."

They rose, and he slipped his arm around her waist.

"Did you ever hear," he said, whispering in her ear, "that Cleveland is very beautiful during the wintertime?"

"Uh . . . no. I never heard that."

"Well, don't you think you ought to judge for yourself?"

She smiled gently and nodded.

17

Evelyn MacMillan was in Cleveland, and in love, and only the latter could explain the former.

It strained her artistic sensibilities to their limits to find anything aesthetically pleasing about this cold gray city. She supposed a stark watercolor of this bleak urban landscape would have its merits; a nice place to paint, but she wouldn't want to live there.

But, nonetheless, she was considering doing just that.

She had accompanied Eliot from Chicago on Thursday of last week, his family matters settled. Other than a brief emotional outpouring just hours after he learned of his mother's passing, he had remained stoic; but Ev knew he wasn't emotionless: he was just holding it all in.

The death of his mother had affected Eliot deeply, whether he admitted it or not, whether he expressed it or not, and knowing that gave Ev an irresistible urge to be supportively at his side.

So here she was in Cleveland, of all places. Where she had, of all things, spent the afternoon interviewing with Frank Darby at the May Company and Charles Bradley at Higbee's for a position as fashion illustrator. And both gentlemen had indicated that some work, if not a full-time position, would be available to her.

She knew very well that Eliot had pulled some strings for her. That didn't bother her: She knew that all the string-pulling in the world couldn't get an artist a job if said artist's portfolio wasn't up to snuff. And hers was up to snuff, and then some. She was an independent woman, but she didn't mind having a man open a door for her.

And she could see, from their evening at the country club this Saturday past, that this particular man was well liked and well-entrenched in the upper social circles of Cleveland (though till Saturday night the notion of Cleveland having any "society" had never occurred to her). There was no question that Eliot was an influential public official, and even more famous here than in his native Chicago.

He had prominence and power and fame, and she liked that. Moreover, she liked him. She found him enormously attractive, even if he wasn't storybook handsome or flashy. There was a boyishness about him that made her want to mother him. He had been, after all, a motherless child from the very start of their love affair.

And, though just a little over a week old, it was a love affair, all right, in full swing. Nothing boyish about Eliot in that department.

And as unglamorous, as cheerless, as colorless as this city was, there was one small pocket of it she had already come to cherish: King Eliot's castle. She had fallen immediately in love with the turreted boathouse at Clifton Lagoon in that posh pocket of posh Lakewood. It had a barren sort of beauty, this weathered graystone palace, the gray-blue of its front-yard lagoon broken only by the occasional wave and the luxury yachts moored there.

Best of all, atop its two sturdy stories was a squat tower, which Eliot had already promised her for a studio.

My, this had gotten serious fast.

Today, she had met him at City Hall, just after five, but he hadn't got away till seven; she had amused herself till then, wandering the stately building, taking in particularly the famous painting *The Spirit of '76*, not the original but a copy by Archibald Willard himself. Perhaps Cleveland was cultured after all.

Now, after an informal bite of supper at the Theatrical

Grill, they were in the black Ford sedan with its personalized plates, EN-1, and she was sitting close to him, though both his hands were on the wheel. His eyes were not always on the road.

They looked like twins, though quite by accident, both wearing tan camel's hair coats and leather gloves; her jaunty felt hat, with its turned-down brim, echoed his snap-brim fedora, although hers was wine color and his a dark green.

The windscreen wipers were on. It was snowing, gently. But even the snow in Cleveland seemed a sooty gray.

"Why don't you put your arm around me, you big lug?" she said.

They were moving west on Lakeside, passing by the courthouse.

He gave her a smile that managed to be both sour and sweet. "I'm the safety director of the city, doll. I have an example to set."

She laughed. "You do insist on calling me that, don't you."

"What?"

"'Doll.' It's so corny."

"I seem to recall you calling me a 'big lug' not so long ago."

"You got me," she said, and held up her wrists, locked together. "Slap on the cuffs."

"You look like you might not hold up too well under the third-degree."

"Why don't you get me back to that boathouse and see, copper?"

He smiled at her again, a small one-sided smile, and put his eyes back on the road. He turned left on West Ninth Street, and glanced up at the rearview mirror. His eyes tightened. So did his lips.

"Is something wrong?" she asked.

"No."

"Eliot, what is it?"

"Probably nothing. That car behind us, that just cut off from that side street..."

"What about it?"

"It doesn't have a license plate."

"What does that mean?"

"Probably nothing," he said lightly, smiling again, but his eyes kept flicking back to the rearview mirror.

She turned to look, and he touched her arm, gently. "Don't," he said.

"You could call on your police radio or whatever it is, couldn't you?"

"It's nothing. He's fallen back. There's two cars between now. It's nothing."

Her heart was pounding. Cleveland didn't seem so dull all of a sudden.

"Coming up," Eliot said, "is proof that this fair city does have its cultural qualities."

He was nodding to a massive concrete-and-steel bridge spanning the Cuyahoga and its industrial area; with its many arches and abutments, it did have a certain skeletal beauty.

"Largest double-decker concrete bridge in the world," he said, with what might have been pride but probably was dry humor. And he was still looking in the rearview mirror.

"How very interesting," she said, and she moved closer to him, not for comfort, but to get a better look at that mirror herself.

Eliot guided the sedan up the ramp onto the upper level of the bridge, the screech of the streetcars below cutting the air like a wounded animal's cry. There were four lanes of traffic up here, moderate traffic at the moment; the pedestrian walkways on either side weren't getting any business at all right now.

The landscape below was a gloomy one—the Flats, Eliot called it; a long freighter heavy with iron ore was moving upriver, heading for one of the steel mills, no doubt. Looking down at the Cuyahoga, which seemed yellow under the glimmer of city lights, she was amazed by this city's lack of regard for itself. Earlier she'd gotten a load of the lakefront, which was littered with industry, a wasteland of smokestacks and salt mines. Not like back home, where the lake was damn near sacred.

For a moment she forgot about the car behind them.

And when she looked in the rearview mirror, she didn't know what she was looking for.

"What color is it?"

"What color is what?" he asked.

"The car! That's following us."

"I don't think he's following us."

"Is he still back there?"

"Yes. Three cars behind us."

"What color is it, damn it!"

"It's a dark blue Buick sedan."

She looked in the rearview mirror again. She could see the car; it was too far back, and the bridge not well lit enough, for her to make out anything else.

He took one hand off the wheel and patted her leg. "It's nothing," he said. "A man in my line of work learns to be careful."

"The alienists call it 'paranoid.'"

"That, too."

"Eliot. I think he's moving up."

"He's just passing. We're going a little slow and the cars behind us aren't passing. He is. Nothing to get excited about."

"He's coming up. He's coming up on us!"

"Please, Ev. Easy. It's just a car. It's just . . . get down! Down!"

She ducked down on the seat.

"Eliot, what is it?"

"I saw a glint of what might be metal. Get on the floor. Get on the floor!"

She got on the floor, up in front of the rider's seat, as low as she could, against and under the dash.

"He's pulling alongside," Eliot said. "Brace yourself."

Eliot hit the gas pedal and a metallic staccato thunder shook the night, and the car. The windows on Eliot's side shattered, like brittle ice, emptying in on Eliot.

"Eliot!"

"Stay down! I'm fine . . ."

He was slouched behind the wheel, head up only barely enough to see as he drove; the roar of both accelerating vehicles replaced the monotone chatter of what she supposed was a machine gun, as they raced along the bridge.

"Do you have a *gun?*" she shouted.

"No," he said. "Just stay down. These doors are heavy—hard for bullets to penetrate."

What a comfort *that* was.

"I'm going to ram him. Hold on!"

She braced her hands against the underside of the dash and the car swung over into the next lane and there was a metallic crunch as their car sideswiped the adversary vehicle, jolting it and her.

Then Eliot swerved back, and the *tat-tat-tat-tat-tat-tat* resumed, landing up toward the front, she thought, across the side of the engine hood.

Eliot hit the pedal again, and the car lurched forward, but just as suddenly he hit the brakes and slid with a smack against the guardrail to the right, jostling Ev, shaking her like a child by an angry abusive parent.

The sedan stopped up against that rail, and Eliot was sitting up now, calling in on the hand microphone of his police radio. He let go with a flurry of words, which she was in no shape to hear, but it did register that there was almost no emotion in his voice, other than perhaps a cold, tight anger.

He clicked off the mike and looked down at her with concern, the emotion finally coming through.

"Are you all right?"

"I don't know. I honestly don't know."

He reached his hand out. "They're gone. They've gone on and won't be back. You're safe."

She took his hand and allowed him to pull her up on the seat. There was glass everywhere, particularly on him, tiny bits of it, flecking his shoulders like dandruff, but also bigger pieces. The windscreen, she saw, had not been touched. The motor was still running.

"Why didn't you get hit," she said, "when they shot out that side window?"

"They didn't shoot it out," he said. "It broke from the impact. I'd already ducked down, so the gunner aimed for the door. Hard to shoot through a bulky car door, even with a Thompson."

"You mean, we were safe as long as we were down low?"

"No. A third of the bullets would make it through, probably, and a third of those would do damage. He probably fired off a hundred rounds."

She swallowed. "Why are we alive?"

"He hit behind us, and in front of us. Tommy gun's not much for hitting a moving target when you're shooting from a moving vehicle. He was stupid—a shotgun would've made a lot more sense."

"Oh, really? A shotgun would've made sense."

He smiled at her, touched her face. "Let's get out of this thing before we cut ourselves to pieces on this broken glass."

Then they were standing on the bridge, in the chilly night with its sooty snow drifting like dust motes, traffic having screeched to a halt. Eliot's assessment of the damage was correct: the pattern of bullet holes—nasty round holes that puckered away the paint around them, groupings so close that some of the holes gathered into larger, gaping ones—were along the rear door and up along the side of the front left fender. But not a tire was flat.

He brushed the glass fragments off him with gloved hands and then he grinned at her sheepishly and said, "Does Cleveland still strike you as dull as dishwater?"

"No," she said, and she grabbed onto him, hugging his arm. Then he took her into his arms and in front of God and Cleveland and the startled motorists making their way around the stalled vehicle, he kissed her slowly and passionately.

"I'm sorry," he said, still holding her. "I'm so sorry."

"Don't be sorry," she said. Her fear was slipping

away; she was now caught in an ephemeral moment of romance and melodrama that she would remember fondly till her dying day.

"Somebody's going to be sorry," he said. And his face was hard, now; nothing boyish about it.

Sirens slashed the stillness.

Soon two squad cars were on the scene, and she leaned against the guardrail, feeling strangely exhausted and oddly distanced, as Eliot gave the details to the uniformed officers. The young, towheaded detective called Curry pulled up shortly thereafter, rushing up to his "chief," his anxiety as apparent as his devotion.

Eliot filled in Curry, who said, "Did you see who it was?"

"No. It was a man, with a hat slouched down and a plaid scarf over his lower face, like a damn highwayman. That's all I saw, and not very well, at that. That tommy gun was talking."

"But there were two of them?"

"Yes. He had a driver. That's a shift in M.O."

Curry sighed. "No license plate. We'll find the car abandoned in the Flats somewhere, no doubt."

"No doubt. But I want you to start picking up those spent forty-fives. Let's see if we can match this machine gun up with the one that ate Gordon's restaurant and killed Jack Whitehall."

Curry nodded. "Too bad we can't tie it into that incident at the food terminal. We've got three witnesses now, who will come forward and identify Harry Gibson as having shot up that farmer's car, including the farmer himself."

"But without any spent bullets from the terminal shooting, to make comparison, we don't have the link we need."

"I know." The young detective sighed. "Do you want me to close traffic off on this bridge? And treat it like a crime scene?"

"No. That's impractical. Just collect the bullets from

the backseat of my car and take the appropriate field notes."

Curry nodded. "I'm glad to hear you say that. It's too late to preserve the integrity of this as a crime scene, anyway. Too many gawkers have stopped along the way to interfere with the evidence."

Eliot nodded absently.

"Some guy stopped to let his kids out," Curry said, with an amused smirk. "You should have seen those kids fighting over who got those bullets."

That seemed to perk Eliot up. "What?"

"A couple of boys, one about ten, another in his early teens. They were picking up souvenirs."

Eliot snapped his fingers. "That's it! That's how we can get our slugs from the food-terminal shooting!"

"What are you talking about, Chief?"

"There are all kinds of kids around a food market. Kids doing odd jobs, for pennies and produce. Cooler boys. That farmer whose truck got shot up had *his* kid with him."

"So?"

Eliot was smiling; it seemed to Ev an unsettling smile. He was poking his young protégé in the chest with a forefinger.

"Some of those kids picked up souvenirs, too, you can bet. A machine-gunning at the food terminal? Are you kidding? That's a big event."

Now Curry was smiling as well. "You're right! Some of those kids would've picked up a bullet or two, shell casings, as mementos."

Eliot put his hand on the young detective's shoulder, in a fatherly fashion. "Go find those kids, and find those bullets. And then we'll let the Ballistics Unit do their job."

"And then?"

"And then," Eliot said, "I'll do mine."

Listening to this conversation, watching the two men speak, Ev felt almost jealous. Not of young Curry, but of Eliot's job itself. She doubted she could ever be as important in his life as it was.

But she was going to give it the old college try.

He came over to her and said, "I can get us a lift back to the boathouse. How does that sound?"

"Better than machine-gun fire," she said, and smiled, and took his arm.

18

Coming down the steep incline of Commercial into the Flats, Ness could see the smokestacks of Republic Steel against the horizon to the southeast. The holstered .38 under his left arm was a reminder of his last official venture into this section of town. To his far right loomed the Lorain-Carnegie Bridge, over the shoulder of which peered the ever-present Terminal Tower. Hard to believe this dirty, shabby district was only ten minutes from downtown.

Riding with him on this cold, cloudy late afternoon, in the new sedan bearing the old EN-1 plates, were detectives Albert Curry, in front, and Will Garner, in back. In a separate car following were Bob Chamberlin, Captain Savage, and a plainclothes officer from Savage's Vandal Squad.

Ness drove along West Fourth, into a warehouse district nestled in a loop of the Cuyahoga, the twisting, oily-yellow river seemingly all around them, glimmering in the overcast day's filtered light. Acme Brothers Glass Works was a big sprawling brick building, with a windowed area at right and a loading dock at left. Ness pulled in so that his sedan was concealed by one of the several parked glass-company trucks. The white trucks had slanting side panels bearing racks with rubber pads and holders designed to hold plate glass.

Chamberlin pulled in alongside Ness; the second car was also hidden by the parked plate-glass trucks. Chamberlin, Curry, Savage, Savage's plainclothes dick, and Garner gathered around Ness like a football team huddling about their quarterback. The big Indian investigator was smoking a cigar, and in his hands was a sawed-off shotgun. It wasn't regulation, but Ness knew better than to complain; that gun had been on many a Chicago campaign.

Ness smiled blandly and said, "I don't anticipate any shooting, but I want you to have your guns out."

The men got their guns out—except for the already-armed Garner, of course.

"I'm going in alone," Ness said. "And if you should hear shooting within, don't come in after me."

There were expressions of confusion all around—except, of course, for Garner, who only smiled a little. He'd been on more raids with Ness than the rest of these men put together.

"It's vital that you keep all the exits blocked," Ness continued. "It's a fairly big facility, with a lot of ways out; fortunately, the windows are mostly too high for exiting."

"He might get to the roof," Garner said. "Warehouses have lofts and such. Ladders up to storage areas."

"True," Ness said, "but we're not expected. If our man bolts, he'll bolt immediately, and for one of the exits. So wait until I'm inside, and then deploy yourselves accordingly."

Ness did not have his gun in hand. He wore the tan camel's hair topcoat with his badge pinned to the lapel; the badge was glittering gold and it said CITY OF CLEVELAND—DIRECTOR OF PUBLIC SAFETY. He walked calmly across the graveled loading dock and parking area and went up the half flight of stairs and inside.

There was no vestibule, no reception area, just an open room with only a single counter separating visitors from the half-dozen desks where secretaries and various office personnel were at work.

Ness spoke to the nearest office worker, who was typing up a form or a bill of some kind. A plain woman of about thirty, wearing glasses, she seemed startled and annoyed all at once.

"May I speak to the office manager?"

"In what regard?"

Ness tapped his gold badge. "Police business."

"Just a moment," she said, trying for indignation but seeming mostly unsettled. She rose and walked briskly off, a small-busted, wide-hipped woman in a white blouse and black skirt.

Ness glanced to the left, where the warehouse was. A double doorway was marked NO ADMITTANCE. He returned his gaze to the office area, where he found every eye trained on him, but only for a moment, as the workers returned nervously to their work, all of them having the guilty look that most innocent people have when police intrude into their lives.

The office manager was a man in a vest and loosened tie and rolled-up shirt-sleeves; he was perhaps fifty, stocky and balding, with a rumpled face that had a cigar stuck in its skeptical mouth.

"What sort of police business?" the man asked.

No niceties; just right into it.

"I understand Harry Gibson works for you."

"That's right. What about it?"

"Where is he?"

"What's this about?"

"I have a warrant for his arrest."

"Is that right?" The skeptical mouth twisted into a smile. "But do you have a search warrant for Acme Glass?"

"No. But I will leave armed police at every exit while I go get one. And when I come back, I'll have more than a search warrant. I'll have photographers and reporters from every paper in town. Maybe you'd like the free publicity."

The mouth lost its skepticism; in fact, it went slack, the cigar clinging to the moisture in one corner.

"Well?" Ness said.

"He's in the warehouse. He has a desk he sits at."

"Is it in an office?"

"No. Right out in the open. I only have one office back there, and the warehouse manager needs it. Harry, uh . . ."

"What?"

The man shrugged; now he seemed embarrassed. "Harry doesn't do much around here, really."

Ness laughed shortly. "What a shock."

Ness walked to the double doors, then turned and saw the office manager standing at a desk with a phone in hand.

"Give Big Jim my best regards," Ness said pleasantly. "And tell him he's next."

The office manager tasted his tongue and nodded, but did not put down the phone.

Ness unbuttoned his topcoat. He unbuttoned his suitcoat underneath. He touched the gun under his arm, half withdrew it from the holster, just to loosen the weapon from the leather binding, and put it back in place. Then he went in.

Off to the left was the slant of the loading-dock area, with three large garage doors. Immediately he passed the warehouse manager's office; the manager—or so he assumed, as the fellow was wearing a shirt and tie—was talking to two men in work denims. All three wore metal helmets. The manager noticed Ness walking by and stepped out of his office with a look of irritation and concern.

Before the man could speak, Ness tapped his badge with a forefinger and said, quietly, "Harry Gibson."

The manager made a disgusted face—more out of distaste for Gibson, Ness thought, than anything else—and pointed off into the warehouse area.

Ness moved past a wall of pegboard where various tools hung, past the loft over the manager's office—a loft stacked with truck tires and boxes—and into a world of wood, metal, and glass.

It was a vast high-ceilinged room, cement floor, brick walls. Wood crates of plate-glass sheets, stored upright in metal framework bins, were arranged in rows, with aisles between them, with occasional open work areas where metal-hatted glaziers were cutting glass on large workbenches while others tended a massive machine with rollers on which large plate-glass sheets were being washed. Some of the metal frameworks were two-story affairs, with sheets stored sideways; steel ladders, some of them on rollers, were here and there. The warehouse was a warren of metal framework and wooden racks and glinting green-edged glass.

Looking up, Ness saw a gridwork of metal beams and bars and pipes, with several pulley systems designed to unload trucks and move massive crates of glass. Handcarts with glass sheets roped onto two-sided padded racks, which formed tight upside down V's, were lined up like autos in traffic, though occasionally a dolly, loaded or not, was stalled out in an aisle. But mostly there was row upon row of stacked, crated, racked glass sheets.

It was a big facility, but Cleveland was a big city, and this one warehouse had a good share of that city's glass business in its pocket; no wonder Big Jim Caldwell's income was in six figures.

Toward the back of the building, behind an open area where glaziers were assembling windows—the sound of their hammering not unlike that of machine-gun fire—sat Harry Gibson, at a desk on which his feet were up. He was reading *The Police Gazette*; his lips were moving. It occurred to Ness that, oddly, he had never seen a police-man reading *The Police Gazette*. Gibson, whose metal hard hat was on his desk next to a cup of coffee, was wearing denims and work shoes, like the other workers, but his looked unused, like his conscience.

"Hello, Harry."

Gibson looked away from the pin-up photo he was perusing to regard his visitor. His eyes narrowed; his lumpy face tightened in thought and aggravation.

"What the hell do you want?"

"A word with you."

"I'm busy, Ness. Go make your headlines at some-body else's expense."

"You do look busy, Harry. By the way, you're under arrest."

Gibson sighed heavily, as if to say, *Oh, brother;* then he grinned. His teeth were a pale yellow, like sweet corn. He hauled his feet down off the desk. He stood. He was a big, brawny son of a bitch, at least two inches taller than Ness.

"What chickenshit charge is it this time, Ness?" Gibson said, sneering down at the detective. "Breaking windows? Tossing stink bombs?" He shook his head, his greased-back brown hair as motionless as if painted on his scalp. "Don't you ever get tired of bum-rapping the labor movement?"

Ness took several steps and stood very close to Gibson; he could smell the man's boozy breath. With a small smile, in a quiet voice, Ness said, "My girl was in the car."

Gibson, shaken, stepped back a little, not enjoying having Ness right up on him like that, staring up at him coldly. "W-What . . . what are you—"

"My girl could have been killed. She was in the car with me when you went duck hunting on the bridge with your tommy gun. That was unwise of you, Harry."

"You're crazy—you're a goddamn crazy man!"

"We matched the bullets, Harry. We matched them all—we can tie you to the food terminal, and Gordon's restaurant, and Jack Whitehall, and the shooting on the High-Level Bridge."

Gibson's eyes were jumpy; he began to sputter. "Prove it, big man. Who's gonna testify against me? Did *you* see me?"

"We've got witnesses who'll testify, Harry. But we won't need them. We went through your apartment this afternoon. We had a search warrant. We went through your garage. We found the gun, Harry. We've got the gun. And now we've got you."

Gibson grabbed the coffee cup off his desk and hurled its contents in Ness's face; the sting of alcohol hit Ness's eyes, and he rubbed them dry with a coat sleeve while with his other hand yanking the thirty-eight from the shoulder holster.

But when he could see again, it was in time only to glimpse Gibson hightail it around the corner of a wall of crated, racked sheet glass.

Ness followed, but as he rounded the corner, he

stopped short before running headlong into a dolly loaded with glass, left there to trip him up by Gibson, who he could see sprinting down the aisle, amazingly fast for a big man.

"Stop or I'll shoot," Ness yelled, and Harry didn't, and Ness did.

The bullet missed Harry, hitting just behind him, the shot echoing through the warehouse, all but drowning out the crash of the plate glass it spiderwebbed. Workers were scrambling for the loading dock area and those big garage doors.

Gibson ducked around another corner.

This time Ness doubled back around, so as not to run into any more traps. But when he entered the aisle, he found it empty. He crawled through a space between the crates in the metal rack that was the aisle's left wall and entered the next aisle, the final one on that side of the building. But no Harry.

Down at the end of the aisle was a ladder on wheels. Perhaps if he climbed up on that, he'd have a vantage point from which he could spot Gibson. He knew if Gibson made for any one of the exits, the men outside would nail the bastard. No need to panic.

Ness moved quickly down the aisle, not quite running, not wanting to make that much noise, and when he heard the scraping sound above him, he pulled back. The sheets of glass rained down and shattered before him, ricocheting off the cement, hitting the floor like a clumsy waitress spilling all the dishes in the world.

But he'd covered his face, and none of the large fragments had flown to find him, and he fired upward, to the sound of more breaking glass, and of Gibson up above, scrambling.

Ness turned the corner to see that another of the ladders on wheels was standing in this aisle, mid-way, almost close enough for Gibson—up on the second level, standing in a half-empty bin—to reach out and pull over. He was stretching out a hand for it when Ness called out.

"Hold it, Harry!"

And Harry, looking toward Ness, who was aiming the revolver up at him, lost his balance.

He pitched into the metal ladder, which scooted away on its wheels as Gibson careened off and tumbled backward and landed, hard, on his back, on the multiple edges of roped, upright sheets of glass below. His mouth opened to cry out, but no cry ever emerged.

He was pinned there, the massive sharp edge of stacked glass poking through him like the point of a giant's sword. He wriggled, caught like a bug, but he seemed dead already—perhaps these were death spasms. Ness, feeling as detached as a surgeon, stood looking up at the dangling, impaled Gibson. Blood soaked the denim shirt and dripped heavily to the cement floor. Eyes open, head tilted to one side, body slack, chest pierced, Harry Gibson had found a way to beat the murder rap.

Ness went to the nearest exit and opened the door. An anxious Albert Curry stepped inside.

"I heard the shots. Are you okay?"

"Yes," Ness said. "Go round everybody up and come in the front way."

Soon his crew was around him, standing in the aisle looking up at the punctured Gibson.

"That's a new one," Will Garner said, uncharacteristically impressed. "How did you manage it?"

"I didn't want him dead," Ness said.

"Sure you did," Garner said, shotgun cradled in his arms. "You would have rather it been in an electric chair, is all."

"We needed that son of a bitch," Ness said.

Curry nodded glumly. "Without him, the link to McFate and Caldwell is gone."

"Unless maybe we can find whoever was driving for him," Savage said, "the night he shot up your car on the bridge."

"We don't have any leads on the driver," Ness said grimly. "None at all."

Chamberlin put a hand on Ness's shoulder; the smile under the tiny mustache was kind, reassuring. "Eliot—

let's look at the bright side: a murderer is dead. And after the work you've done—we've *all* done, these past four months—you've got plenty to go to the grand jury with, on racketeering and extortion charges."

Ness was nodding. "You're right. It's time to put those bastards out of business, and behind bars, where they damn well belong."

Everyone nodded. The sound of Gibson's dripping blood seemed to make it unanimous.

19

On the Monday just prior to Christmas, in the union headquarters in the six-story building on East Seventeenth Street, little holiday cheer was in evidence.

In the outer office, where Big Jim Caldwell's attractive brunette secretary sat typing, a small fir trimmed with tinsel and red and green electric lights was perched upon a small table, but there were no gifts under the tree.

And in Big Jim's office there was no tree, no tinsel, no cheer whatsoever. On this occasion it was Big Jim who was pacing, while Little Jim sat behind his partner's desk, drinking whiskey from a water glass. Anger clenched Caldwell's round face; McFate slouched in the chair, with an even more doleful expression than usual.

"I feel so goddamn helpless," Caldwell said.

McFate said nothing.

Caldwell stopped and gestured with two open hands. "There's got to be *some* way to stop this thing."

McFate shrugged.

Caldwell paced. He knew McFate would have nothing trenchant to contribute, but he couldn't keep his frustration inside; he had to voice it.

But he knew, too, that McFate's silence was an appropriate response. There had been nothing that could be done to squelch the grand-jury inquiry. It had been too sweeping a probe, with more than one hundred witnesses called, including the two Jims themselves. How do you intimidate that many witnesses? How do you even keep track of them? For that matter, with the secrecy that Ness and Prosecutor Cullitan had imposed, how could you know *how* a witness had testified? You couldn't tell the betrayers from the faithful without a scorecard—and there were no fucking scorecards!

Then Little Jim surprised Caldwell and spoke up.

"If they get an indictment," Little Jim said, swirling whiskey in his glass, "that means a jury trial. No more of this behind-closed-doors grand-jury shit. No more ban on reporters. We'll know what's going on. We'll know who to bribe and who to put the fear of God in."

Caldwell stopped pacing. He put his hands on his hips and smiled. "You know, you're right, bucko. It's too late to worry about the grand jury. It's spilt milk. But we can show Ness and Cullitan that their tactics won't work in a *real* trial in an old-fashioned American open courtroom."

"If there even *is* a trial," McFate said, forcing a small smile onto his dour face. "I don't think Ness's got enough evidence to get an indictment. That grand jury's been meeting for over a month, and nothing's come of it."

"On that count I'm afraid you're wrong, boyo," Caldwell said, shaking his head. "They've talked to over one hundred witnesses."

"That just backs me up, lad. They wouldn't have to work so hard if something was really turning up. Do you really think somebody like Vernon Gordon is going to spill? He's still paying off, isn't he, to the window washers union?"

"Yes," Caldwell admitted.

McFate shrugged again. "See? This is a pain in the ass, knowing they're trying to nail us but not knowing what's going on exactly and not being able to do a damn thing about it. But it's not going to amount to nothing."

"I wish I could share your confidence, laddie-buck," Caldwell said, sighing. "I think we'll be indicted on general principles. Cullitan won't need a shred of damn evidence. That grand jury won't have the guts to return a no-bill against Ness's say-so."

McFate grunted matter-of-factly and sipped at his glass. "So then if there is a trial—and there won't be—we put the pressure on, where the witnesses are concerned. Police protection only goes so far, you know."

"We don't have Harry Gibson anymore, remember," Caldwell said, lifting an eyebrow. "And this is no time to be bringing in somebody new for that kind of thing."

McFate's optimism seemed to fade. "Too bad. We could use Harry along about now."

Caldwell's laugh was short and sharp. "Are you joking? Losing Harry is the one good thing that's happened to us lately. At least we got home free, where Whitehall's concerned."

McFate considered that and nodded, no longer missing Harry.

In the outer office, a door slammed.

Caldwell looked at McFate; McFate looked at Caldwell.

Loud voices, the words themselves muffled by the closed door, were echoing out there; a commotion was brewing.

And before either Jim had a chance to go and check up on it, the brunette secretary, looking flustered and a little scared, squeezed in the inner office, having opened the door only barely, closing it behind her. It was as if a wild beast were on the other side.

Wide-eyed, breathless, she said, "There are some men here to see you, Mr. Caldwell."

"Police?"

"No," she said, shaking her head vigorously. "Some men from the union. Some of the members."

The door behind her pushed open, pushing her rudely out of the way. She scurried to a neutral corner as half a dozen men in work denims and winter jackets poured in. At their head was Joe McFarlin, a shovel-jawed six-foot-two bruiser, a trouble-making roughneck as far as Caldwell was concerned.

"We're seizing these headquarters in the name of the rank and file," McFarlin said.

"The hell you are!" Caldwell said. "This is my private office. If you want an appointment with me, you—"

McFarlin thumped Caldwell in the chest with a finger

as thick as the base of a pool cue. "I want nothing from you but your ouster, you son of a bitch."

McFate moved in between them, placed a hand on both their chests. "Joe. We've always gotten along, haven't we? If you have any complaints, there's ways to go about it. Procedures—"

"Fuck procedures," McFarlin said, brushing off McFate's hand like an insect. "The procedure we're going to follow is the one that works best for union guys like us. A sit-down strike."

"A *strike?*" Caldwell said, incredulous. "How the hell do you strike against your own *union?*"

"Watch," McFarlin said. And he nodded to one of the men behind him, who exited and within moments came back with more men, pouring in from the hallway through the outer office to invade Caldwell's sanctuary.

Soon, in excess of forty men had squeezed into the modest room, their mortar-splattered shoes scuffing the floor. The air hung with the smell of sweat, strong tobacco (both chewed and smoked), and booze breath. Caldwell's secretary scurried out and nobody tried to stop her, but most watched her go, appreciating the view.

"Make yourself at home," McFarlin told the men.

And all forty-some representatives of the rank and file sat down. On the floor.

"These are the union business offices," Caldwell said, almost yelling, moving through the seated crowd, searching for space and a sympathetic face. "If you want a meeting, go down to the union hall—that's what it's for."

McFarlin, who other than the two Jims was the only man still standing, shouted over the heads of his fellows. "What about meetings you promised to call, Caldwell, that never got called? What about elections that were supposed to be held but were postponed till never?"

Caldwell said, "We can discuss all that, but not like this. This is an illegal meeting, contrary to union rules—"

"We've had our fill of your 'rules' *and* your 'rule,'" McFarlin said. "You and McFate and your henchmen have been usurping the power of the union long enough. Well, we're going to stage a sit-in campaign between now and three o'clock tomorrow afternoon, at which time we've called a rump meeting to elect officers to take your place."

Caldwell laughed. "You'll fall apart in an hour."

McFarlin smiled nastily. "We've got a majority of the two thousand members of the union behind us, Jim. And two hundred volunteers who are going to work in eight-hour shifts."

McFate said, "You're not going to get away with this, lads. Do you think the AFL is going to allow—"

"Sit-downs? Strikes?" McFarlin laughed. "I think they just might be familiar with those measures. I think they'll approve. Particularly if we find anything at all out of order in your records and files, which we intend to seize and give a thorough going over."

Caldwell's face reddened. "Get out! All of you! God-damn it, I'm warning you!"

"Ralph, Anton," McFarlin said to two of the burliest sit-downers, "show the boys out, would you?"

Within minutes, Big Jim Caldwell and Little Jim McFate found themselves in an unceremonious heap on the sidewalk in front of their building. Their overcoats and hats, in light of the winter day, had been tossed on the pile. McFarlin, Ralph, and Anton stood with smiles and folded arms, blocking the entryway.

Neither Jim had quite gotten himself up off the pavement when the sedan with the EN-1 license plates pulled into an empty space not far from where they were sprawled.

Ness, hands in the pockets of his tan camel's hair topcoat, the sun winking off the gold badge on his lapel, approached them with a pleasant expression, his breath smoking in the chill afternoon air. Coming up behind him was Detective Albert Curry, the smug little bastard who'd turned up the heat on the two Jims when they were stuck in the lockup with those bums that time.

"You boys lose something?" Ness asked. "Maybe I could assign a detective to help you find it."

Caldwell got up, brushing himself off, putting on his

overcoat, trying to recover his dignity. McFate was rising as well, his long face white with rage.

Caldwell said, "These men assaulted us," and he pointed back to McFarlin and his two cohorts.

"Really?" Ness said. "Were there any witnesses?"

"They stormed our offices," Caldwell said, ignoring the question, "and ejected us from our own premises."

"Who are these fellows?" Ness asked innocently.

"Union members," McFate said, as if that were an obscenity.

Ness shrugged. "Well, that's union headquarters up there, isn't it?"

"They're trespassing, goddamn it!" Caldwell said, shaking his fists, dignity be damned.

"Illegal acts are being committed here," McFate said, just as angry as his partner, but superficially more in control. "You're a policeman. Do something about it."

"Throw the bastards in jail!" Caldwell said. "Earn your goddamn paycheck, Ness!"

"I'm sorry, boys," Ness said, arms folded, smiling placidly. "I can't do that."

"Why in hell not?" Caldwell demanded.

Ness shrugged again, smiled broadly. "Why boys—you know I try never to interfere in union business."

McFarlin and his two cronies hooted with laughter in the background, while Caldwell and McFate burned, and another car pulled in. *Plain Dealer* reporter Sam Wild, with photographer Shorty Philkins in tow, stepped out onto the sidewalk.

"Just happened to be passing by," Wild said. "Something up?"

"You just happened to be passing by," Caldwell said dryly. "With a photographer."

Wild smiled genially. "Slow news day. Actually, there was a rumor that some rank-and-file fellas might attempt a takeover of your local's HQ today. Any truth to that?"

Caldwell was steaming. He looked at Wild, then Ness. "You bastards are behind this, aren't you?"

"Behind what?" Ness asked. "Oh, I've met a couple

of these chaps before. Like Joe McFarlin over there. We met at Jack Whitehall's funeral. Had a nice chat. Joe and Jack were buddies, did you know that?"

Caldwell said nothing to that; he knew better.

But McFate didn't.

"So you're not going to do your job," McFate said. "You're going to let these trespassers get away with it."

"Some people get away with murder," Ness said coldly.

Caldwell touched McFate's arm, hoping to silence him, but his normally taciturn partner continued: "Then you're not going to make an arrest?"

"Oh, I'm going to make an arrest," Ness said. "Two arrests. That's why I'm here. Albert—cuffs, please?"

Curry stepped forward and withdrew two shining pairs of handcuffs from his topcoat pocket.

"Hands behind you, boys," Ness said.

"You're arresting *us*?" McFate said.

"Grand jury indicted you both this afternoon. Five counts of blackmail and extortion."

Caldwell and McFate exchanged alarmed glances.

Then McFate summoned a sneer and said, "It won't hold up. You got nothing."

"Nothing," Ness said, "except ninety-seven witnesses who have testified to more than one hundred instances of blackmail, extortion, and general conspiracy aimed at Cleveland's business community. . . of course, my investigation isn't through yet. I may turn something up yet, you never know. Snap 'em on, Detective Curry."

Curry snapped on the cuffs behind the backs of the two Jims.

"Sorry, boys," Curry said. "We don't have the budget for a brass band and silk top hats for you."

As the two were being walked toward the EN-1 sedan, reporter Wild was asking a few questions.

"What's your purpose here today, Mr. McFarlin?"

"Overthrowing a dictatorship," McFarlin said, smiling tightly, arms folded over a massive chest. "We've tried for several months to get a regular election, but we've been blocked by Caldwell, McFate, and their attorney. We expect to keep up our sit-in at least until tomorrow, when we'll hold an election, junk the former constitution, and draft a new one along democratic lines."

"How about you, Mr. Ness? Anything to say to the press before you haul those two away?"

Ness, about to get into the sedan, turned and said, "Ask Mr. McFarlin and some of his compatriots what *they* think of my efforts in the area of labor. This investigation began with complaints from businessmen. But since then, since the grand jury convened, my office has been flooded with calls and letters from rank-and-file union members. They've told us how union business agents like Caldwell and McFate sit in their offices and instead of sending legitimate union members on jobs, send patronage punks who don't do the work well, discrediting the name of union labor, thumbing their noses at employers, who don't dare fire the loafers because if they do, the job will get shut down by a strike. That sounds like a crime to me—which is where I come in."

"Eliot Ness, friend of labor," Wild said archly.

"No," Ness said. "Enemy of lice like them."

And he nodded toward the glowering Caldwell and morose McFate as Curry pushed them bodily into the backseat of the sedan.

THREE

March 12, 1938

20

CITY OF CLEVELAND
Office of the Mayor

March 12, 1938

Director Eliot Ness,
Department of Public Safety,
City Hall

Re: Caldwell and McFate Case

Dear Eliot:

Confirming and developing my oral statement immediately following my receipt of the news of the conviction of Caldwell and McFate, this letter is to express to you my official and personal appreciation of the exceptional public service which you rendered in this case.

This case and the long investigation leading up to it has dealt with one of the worst conditions in Cleveland. It has been a major purpose of this administration to put an end to extortion and related forms of racketeering in Cleveland. From the first day that you joined us, you have in a quiet and modest way led the attack on this evil. The conviction of Caldwell and McFate marks a major victory in the battle, and I believe marks the turning point in our campaign to drive out the rackets.

This particular case presented every kind of difficulty, culminating in the hard fought trial itself. I am deeply grateful to you for the competent, patient, and long, continued hard work that you did in connection with it. I know that not only Cleveland but the nation is indebted to you for the result attained.

This has been by no means an attack on organized labor as such, as the service which you have rendered has been a service for the benefit of industry, labor, and the public at large.

I hope that you enjoy your well-earned vacation and will return to your duties here, ready to continue the drive with your usual vigor and with increased assurance of success.

With warmest personal regards,

Harold H. Burton
Mayor

After reading it for a third time, Eliot Ness, seated at his rolltop desk in his office, folded the letter and returned it to its envelope. He buzzed Wanda, who entered promptly, steno pad in hand.

"No dictation," Ness said, with a gentle smile. "Just another souvenir. Paste this in the scrapbook, will you?"

Wanda smiled tightly and took the letter. "We may need a separate volume for '38, Mr. Ness. The wires and clippings are starting to pour in from all over the country."

"Start a new volume, then," Ness said. "We want to give McFate and Caldwell their due."

"Yes sir," she said, and exited.

He blew out some air, and leaned back in the swivel chair. He was pleased with the response, locally and nationally, to the conviction of the "boys." The public statements of approval from union circles was perhaps the most gratifying—from the UAW president in Detroit to the national AFL rep. Even his old adversary George Owens of SWOC had been complimentary: "We are in back of Ness one hundred percent. The labor movement must be kept clean to survive."

Of course, Owens had used the occasion to nudge Ness publicly about investigating industry, as well, who "have sent their stool pigeons, thugs, finks, spies, and agents to disrupt the labor movement." And he had a point.

But Ness did not feel smug, or even proud. He did not feel much of anything except exhausted, and a weekend in a cabin near Lake Geneva, Wisconsin, with Ev MacMillan, should be just what the doctor ordered. He was taking an evening train to Chicago, and intended to put unions, rackets, and Cleveland out of his mind for the next week.

The trial had been hard fought, as the Mayor indicated, and Ness had spared no manpower in protecting the witnesses—the local ones who were put up in hotels or guarded at home, as well as those who came in by plane and train from Milwaukee, Boston, St. Paul, Detroit, Kansas City, Buffalo, Syracuse, Chicago, and Columbus. And he had gotten the local papers to cooperate in extending his grand-jury press-photographer ban to the trial itself.

Of course, Caldwell and McFate had had a few tricks left up their sleazy sleeves. On the second day of the trial, Ness got a tip from Joe McFarlin that an attempt to fix one of the jurors was in the wind; a Nitti man had come in from Chicago with fifty thousand dollars in the kitty, to use in reaching a woman on the jury by way of her husband, who had business connections with Acme Brothers Glass.

Ness informed Prosecutor Cullitan, who dismissed the juror without disclosing he knew of the bribe-in-the-works, replacing the juror with an alternate. Judge Cortlett, hard-nosed and refreshingly honest for Cleveland, was also informed by Ness, after which His Honor sequestered the jury for the remainder of the trial.

Caldwell and McFate kept trying, though; they put together a thirty-grand defense fund. They brought in labor leaders from other cities as character witnesses. They testified coolly and even charmingly in their own behalf, both claiming never to have been in the same room before with star prosecution witness Vernon Gordon.

Midway through the trial, defense attorney Corrigan demanded that Eliot Ness be barred from the courtroom because he was "impressing" the jurors with his presence. Judge Cortlett sent the jurors out of the courtroom and quickly denied the motion.

But the jury—six men, six women, primarily labor-union men and the wives of labor-union men—were not buying anything Caldwell and McFate had to sell. The two Jims were found guilty on all five counts, and the judge, God bless his stern countenance, had denied them bail and gave them both ten-year sentences.

At this point Judge Cortlett had taken an extraordinary measure. Speaking of the many precautions safety director Ness and Prosecutor Cullitan had taken to ensure an orderly trial, the judge pointed out that efforts had been made to influence the jury, including the apparent attempt to bribe one juror through her husband, as well as "suspicious incidents" during the trial when friends and even spouses of the jurors took front-row seats in the courtroom, having to be ordered out when they tried to impress the jury members with their friendly, back-slapping attitude toward the defendants.

Because of these incidents, Judge Cortlett ordered the labor leaders sent to the pen immediately following the return of the verdict.

"They are dangerous to the community," the judge said, "and there is reason for witnesses to fear reprisal if these cunning thugs are left at large." The two Jims were in prison at Columbus within eight hours of the guilty verdict.

Wanda stuck her head into the office and said, "I'm sorry to interrupt you, Chief—but there's a woman out here to see you. She doesn't have an appointment."

"Her name?"

"Mrs. Whitehall, she says. Shall I recommend she make an appointment for after you get back?"

"No," Ness said, standing. "Send her in."

Mrs. Whitehall entered. She wore a dark brown hat and a long brown winter coat with a fur collar, apparel that was as quietly attractive as its wearer.

"Please have a seat, Mrs. Whitehall," Ness said, gesturing to one of the conference-table chairs. "Can I take your coat?"

"No," she said. "I won't be staying long."

She stood, clutching her small purse, obviously embarrassed.

"Is there some way I can help you?" Ness asked.

She sighed and smiled awkwardly and said, "I'm here to make a long overdue apology."

"None is needed."

"The night Jack died, I was pretty rough on you."

"No apology is needed, Mrs. Whitehall."

"You weren't to blame for Jack's death. Both Joe McFarlin and your reporter friend Sam Wild have gone out of their way to explain that to me."

"Well . . . that's kind of them, but—"

"Mr. Ness. Please. This isn't easy for me. Joe, and Mr. Wild, made it clear to me that it was the Teamster activity at the food terminal that got Jack killed. And, in fact, it was you who brought Jack's murderer, that horrible man Gibson, to his demise."

Ness felt a wave of weariness wash over him; he sat on the edge of the conference table and said, "Mrs. Whitehall. I didn't intentionally cause the death of Harry Gibson. I was there to arrest him. Frankly, if I'd been more effective in my job, Gibson would've stayed alive, and we would have had the ammunition needed to put his bosses away for life, at least, or better yet, provide them a very hot place to temporarily sit."

She smiled in a manner that crinkled her chin; she seemed to be holding back tears. "You put those terrible men away. You worked very hard, and you put them in prison, this Caldwell and McFate. I followed it in the papers. I even went to the trial on several occasions."

"I know. I noticed you there."

"You've brought their house down. That's what's important. And Joe McFarlin tells me that, well, as he puts it, 'Democracy has been restored to the carpenters and glaziers unions.'"

Ness smiled. "Yes. I understand that's the case. A happy side effect of the investigation."

"Jack would have approved, Mr. Ness. He would have approved your efforts. I know he wouldn't have helped you, otherwise."

Ness couldn't quite bring himself to tell her that he'd essentially blackmailed her husband into helping him, holding that assault charge over Jack's head; but he did feel Whitehall would have been very glad to see Caldwell and McFate out of business and behind bars.

"I'm sorry I slapped you," she said, and, impulsively, she touched his cheek; her hand was cool.

"It's all right," Ness said. "Really."

"Thank you for... accepting my apology."

"None needed. None needed. You know, we may still put Caldwell and McFate away on a murder charge. Gibson had an accomplice who drove a car for him when he tried to shoot me, a while back. If we can find him—"

"It doesn't matter. That would be fine, but you've done quite enough. You've done very well."

The two stood and shared a stiff silence.

Then Ness, almost blurting, said, "You should be proud of your husband, Mrs. Whitehall, what he accomplished with his life."

"Even if you didn't always agree with his methods?"

Ness smiled one-sidedly. "A lot of people don't agree with *my* methods."

Worry touched her face. "Mr. Ness, I'm pleased that you think I should be proud of Jack. But can I suggest one thing? Where labor is concerned, please be careful that your activities are such that my late husband might be proud of *you*."

"Mrs. Whitehall, I'll make every attempt to—"

"No offense, Mr. Ness. But Jack was worried about you... about you living in that fancy castle they've given you, going to nightclubs and country clubs and all with society people. Some day they'll send you a bill, Jack said."

"I'll . . . keep that in mind, Mrs. Whitehall."

She studied him, her tears in check; then, following another impulse, she kissed him on the cheek, where she had once struck him.

Then she was gone, and he stood holding his face, recalling, for some reason, the burning sensation of her months-ago slap.

He sat back down at his desk and was finishing up some paperwork when the intercom buzzed.

"Another visitor without an appointment, sir," Wanda said. She sounded uncharacteristically impressed. "It's Cyril Easton."

So it was time to hear from Cleveland's richest financier. To hear how pleased the city's industrial leaders were with his work on the labor racketeering front. He would accept the compliments graciously, but already he felt unsettled.

"Yes," he said, and shivered. "Well, send him in."

A Tip of the Fedora

As was the case with the two previous Eliot Ness novels, *The Dark City* (1987) and *Butcher's Dozen* (1988), I could not have written this book without the support and advice of my friend and research associate George Hagenauer. George and I have made several research trips to Cleveland, where we visited many of the sites of the action in this novel. We have had numerous sessions at the Western Reserve Historical Society, where the Ness papers are kept. We are both grateful to the helpful personnel at the Historical Society, City Hall municipal reference library, and Cleveland Public Library.

Despite its extensive basis in history, this is a work of fiction, and some liberties have been taken with the facts; the remarkably eventful life of Eliot Ness defies the necessarily tidy shape of a novel, and for that reason I have again compressed time, occasionally reordered events, and used composite characters.

Readers of *Butcher's Dozen* may wish to note that the action of this novel takes place in the period of time filling the gap between sections one and two of that novel.

Some characters, like Sam Wild and Albert Curry, are wholly fictional, although they do have real-life counterparts. Wild represents the many reporter friends of Ness, particularly Clayton Fritchey of the *Press*, who, like the fictional Wild, were assigned to cover Ness full-time; and Ralph Kelly of the *Plain Dealer*, who also covered the City Hall beat.

Big Jim Caldwell and Little Jim McFate are primarily

194

based upon Don Campbell and John McGee, although neither of these notorious convicted felons were ever linked to the death of Arthur Whitelock, the real-life counterpart of Jack Whitehall. Whitelock's murder remains unsolved, although it was obviously tied to his unconventional union-organizing activities.

Harry Gibson is a fictional character, although he has several real-life counterparts in Cleveland labor racketeering circles of the 1930s. Specifically, the extortion racket at the food terminal (and Eliot Ness's investigation thereof) is based closely on fact, although dates have been shifted.

Among the historical figures included here under their real names are Mayor Harold Burton (whose congratulatory letter to Ness as it appears in this novel is a verbatim transcription, with the exception of the substitution of the names "Caldwell and McFate" for "Campbell and McGee"); Chief George Matowitz; Executive Assistant Safety Director Robert Chamberlin; Captain John Savage; Elmer Irey; Judge Alva Cortlett; and Prosecutor Frank T. Cullitan. Mentioned in passing, Frank Nitti and Louis Campagna of course existed; and the names of Eliot Ness's family members used herein are the real ones.

Will Garner, the former "untouchable," is based upon Bill Gardner, who was indeed on Ness's Chicago Capone squad. To my knowledge, Gardner did not work with Ness in Cleveland; but according to several sources, including Oscar Fraley's *Four Against the Mob*, at least one former "untouchable" was on the safety director's staff of investigators. But Ness did not publicize the names of his investigators, who were nicknamed in the press "the unknowns," a name that did not catch on in the manner of "the untouchables." Fraley implies in his slightly fictionalized book (most names are changed, for instance, and some dates) that this staff member was Paul Robsky; but in Robsky's own self-aggrandizing autobiography (co-written with Fraley), *The Last of the Untouchables* (1962), a work which outrageously all but omits Eliot Ness from the story of that famed squad, Robsky makes no mention of having worked in Cleveland. I chose to use Gardner as the basis for the ex-"untouchable" on the Cleveland staff because, frankly, I found him the most interesting of Ness's Chicago investigative team.

Among the fictional characters in this book who have real-life counterparts are George Owens, Frank Darby, Cyril Easton, Mrs. Jack Whitehall, Sergeant Martin Merlo, David Cowley, Evelyn MacMillan, Joe McFarlin, and various incidental characters.

Vernon Gordon is a fictional character designed to represent (but not depict specifically) the Stouffer brothers, Vernon and Gordon. It was the now enormously successful international Stouffer's chain whose Playhouse Square restaurant renovation was the extortion and vandalism target of Don Campbell and John McGee. And it was the cooperation of the Stouffer brothers with Eliot Ness and Prosecutor Cullitan that made the case against Campbell and McGee possible; the Stouffers were indeed the state's star witnesses.

The major research source for this book was the files of various Cleveland newspapers of the day; but a number of books have been consulted as well.

Sources for the labor union aspect of this novel include: *Dynamite* (1934), Louis Adamic; *Labor—Turbulent Years* (1969), Irving Bernstein; *Strike!* (1972), Jeremy Brecher; *As Steel Goes, . . . Unionism in a Basic Industry* (1940), Robert R. R. Brooks; *Teamster Rebellion* (1972), Farrell Dobbs; and *Teamster Politics* (1975), Farrell Dobbs. Also, *Union Guy* (1946) by Edward Fountain provided ideas for the background of Jack Whitehall.

Four Against the Mob (1961) by Oscar Fraley, the co-author with Ness himself of *The Untouchables* (1957), is the only book-length nonfiction work on Ness in Cleveland to date. As mentioned previously, Fraley changed names and did some minor fictionalizing, apparently for legal reasons, and tended not to explore Ness as a man, possibly out of deference to Betty Ness, Ness's widow (and third wife). Nonetheless, his book remains a helpful basic source to me and I am grateful to Mr. Fraley for his work.

Ness has not yet been the subject of a book-length

biography, but a number of excellent articles about him have been written by Cleveland journalists. Undoubtedly the best, and probably the single most helpful source to me, is the article by Peter Jeddick, collected in his *Cleveland: Where the East Coast Meets the Midwest* (1980). Also excellent is the article "The Last American Hero," by George E. Condon, published in *Cleveland Magazine* (August 1987); Condon's book *Cleveland: The Best Kept Secret*, includes a fine chapter on Ness as well, "Cleveland's Untouchable." Also helpful is the unpublished article written in 1983 for the Cleveland Police Historical Society, "Eliot Ness: A Man of a Different Era," by Anthony J. Coyne and Nancy L. Huppert. And extremely valuable is the unpublished, twenty-two-page article written by Ness himself on his Capone days, prepared as background material for co-author/ghost Fraley on *The Untouchables*.

Other references include *Cleveland: Prodigy of the Western Reserve* (1979), George E. Condon; *Yesterday's Cleveland* (1976), George E. Condon; *The Tax Dodgers* (1948), Elmer L. Irey and William J. Slocum; *Cleveland Architecture 1876–1979* (1979), Eric Johannesen; *Scientific Investigation and Physical Evidence* (1959), Leland V. Jones; *Cleveland—Confused City on a Seesaw* (1976), Philip W. Porter; *To Market to Market* (1981), Joanne M. Lewis and John Szilagyi; and *Criminal Investigation* (1974), Paul B. Weston and Kenneth M. Wells.

A tip of the fedora to Joyce Magyar of Mid-American Glass of Davenport, Iowa, for the impromptu tour and for providing helpful information; and to contractor Chuck Bunn, for information regarding the construction business.

Finally, I would like to thank my editor Coleen O'Shea and her associate Becky Cabaza for providing a solid, enthusiastic support system; my agent Dominick Abel, for his counsel and friendship; and my wife Barbara Collins, whose love, help, and support make the work possible.